GRRR!

AN ANTHOLOGY OF EROTICA RELATING TO THE TRAINING OF THE HUMAN DOG

COMPILED AND EDITED BY MICHAEL DANIELS

GRRR!

AN ANTHOLOGY OF EROTICA RELATING TO THE TRAINING OF THE HUMAN DOG

The human dog or pup is a unique creature -
part boy, part dog; part companion,
part servant; protective yet in need of
supervision - a playful guardian to his Master.
Add a compulsion for leather and kink and the mix
becomes even more rewarding - and complicated.

MICHAEL DANIELS

A Boner Book
The Nazca Plains Corporation
Las Vegas, Nevada
2004

ISBN: 1-887895-53-1

Published by: The Nazca Plains Corporation
                       4640 Paradise Rd, Suite 141
                       Las Vegas NV 89109-8000

PUBLISHER'S NOTE:
This is a work of fiction. Names, characters, places, and incidents either are the products of the author's imagination or are used fictitiously, and any resemblance to actual persons, living or dead, business establishments, events or locales is entirely coincidental.

Editor, Kyler O'Leary

Photographer, Corwin

Cover Model, Andy

Illustrations Copyright © by the individual artist: Uli of Berlin

To Contact Author:
            Michael Daniels, leatherDOG, LTD.
            Columbus OH
            SIR@leatherDOG.com

DEDICATION

For jefpup, boy chuck, puppy taber, pug, patrick,
and all those pups who continue to inspire me.

He is your friend, your partner, your defender, your dog.
You are his life, his love, his leader.
He will be yours, faithful and true, to the last beat of his heart.
You owe it to him to be worthy of such devotion.
-- Anonymous

leatherDOG.com

ACKNOWLEDGEMENTS

Special thanks to the loyal readers of leatherDOG.com for their submissions of erotica throughout the history of the site, and for their kind permission to allow their works to be reprinted in this anthology.

These Stories are erotica. As such, they are not meant in any way to be considered as training methods for human pups, but rather only as erotic fiction. We stand by our original work "WOOF" for our tips, tricks and techniques for actual training.

DISCLAIMER

No one associated with the writing, publication, distribution, or sale of this book, or in any other way connected with it, is in any way liable for any damages that may result from engaging in the activities described herein. The reader assumes all risks and associated with his participation.

BDSM in general, and human dog play specifically, is a controversial topic. Do not consider this book a substitute for medical, legal, psychological or professional advice.

Nothing herein is intended to appeal to prurient interests, but is presented to address the psychological and technical aspects of alternative sexual practices between consenting adults.

Finally, please do not consider this text to be the definitive word on human dog training. Seek opinions and advice from others who are experienced and knowledgeable about the topic. Do not automatically and uncritically accept anyone's personal advice, opinion, or techniques regarding human dog play - including those in this book.

TABLE OF CONTENTS

BOWZER

By Mr. Mike

"Bowzer, here boy. Good boy. Good Puppy! Oh yes you like it when I scratch your ears don't you? Now sit boy, quit squirming, sit still for the nice man. He wants to know about you and your life here. There boy, yes boy, go ahead here's your rawhide chewy. Here take it."

I adopted Bowzer last winter. He was at the truck stop, down off the interstate, hustling for rides to nowhere/anywhere. He thought he was turning a trick when I offered him a ride. It was snowing; he was cold so I offered him dinner and a dry bed at my place. He was too cold and miserable to say no. "Right boy?"

Anyway, we got back to the house and I sent him into take a shower while I fixed dinner. That was his last meal at the table. While we ate we talked. He was 19, maybe 5'10", 160 lbs., nice and furry. He had dropped out of school (he's not really bright). He was a bit underweight, (the muscles you see now he put on under my direction). He was running away from home, usual story- drunk and abusive father, missing mother, etc. etc. Running away to no place in particular. "Yeah, boy, chew that rawhide toy." You should see how well he fetches. "Give me the chewy boy, good boy!" Now watch him. "Go fetch boy! Go get it boy." He'll bring it back in a minute, he runs a little slow on all fours. "Run boy, yes that's my good pup!"

The morning after he got here it was clear he didn't want to leave, no place to go, no rush to get there. "Good boy, no you keep it boy. Why don't you lay there in the sun while I talk to the nice man? Go on, be a good pup."

Where were we? Oh yes, the next day - here mind if I have a cigar? Want one? Okay well, why not take it with you...mmm, now that's good - anyway, I'd been wanting a "dog" since I moved out here and started telecommuting. Gets kinda lonely out here. Anyway, after dinner I had him

1

strip down so I could take a look at him, he was a little embarrassed, but stripped anyway and just stood there while I played with his cock and balls and turned him around and poked his ass with my finger. He asked me if he could suck on my cock so I had him kneel here in front of me. I let him suck, but wouldn't let him play with his own very hard dick. Not a great blowjob, but good enough- showed great potential. I realized I really had to pee so holding his head I started pissing in his mouth, and he just swallowed it down, hardly a dribble, course I was peeing nice and slow. He's a lot better at it now, let me show you. "Here boy, open wide boy. Ahhh, good boy, not a drop spilled! Here have a treat boy." I keep chocolate kisses here to give him for treats.

Now where were we, oh that's right his first blow job - anyway, I ended up taking him to bed and wrestled him down for a long leisurely fuck. Actually several long leisurely fucks throughout the night (he stopped wrestling with me after the second or third) and using his ass as a piss dump meant I could stay in my nice warm bed. Anyway, like I said, I'd thought before that a "dog" would be nice and here was my chance. So before I unplugged my cock from his ass I told him what I wanted.

"Okay boy, here's how it's going to work. You're going to be my dog. I'll feed you, fuck you and train you. You'll wear my collar, a butt plug tail and a cock cage. I have a pair of canvas mitts that'll turn your hands into paws." I put my thumb into his mouth to suck on. "Boy, the hardest part is that you will not be allowed to talk or walk. You can bark, whimper, growl, make all kinds of dog sounds and you'll have to stay on all fours. I have a drool gag to help you learn not to speak and a set of shackles that'll keep you from walking upright." I thought I might get a fight out of him instead he smiled, whimpered and enthusiastically nodded yes.

We spent the rest of the day playing and training. That's when I renamed him Bowzer. He got tired of the drool gag but learned that it was going to stay. Oh I took it out so I could piss and planned to leave it out for a while, but he started to say "Thank you." So I slapped his butt with a rolled up newspaper and shoved the gag back in his mouth. Told him, "boy, I told you- NO SPEAKING! You want to thank me? Then do things right and whimper for me." His eyes filled with tears and he whimpered as he rubbed his face against my hand. He was clearly really getting into this dog business. Later in the day I did take the gag out to feed him and he whimpered but didn't speak. There have been a few slips since then, but for the most part he's done okay. "Yes boy, we're talking about you. No stay there for now boy. Good boy."

He learned to 'do his business' out in the back yard. Sure had to shit fast in the snow. I let him pee inside in a quart jar that I held, but he then had to drink it so he tried not to do that often. He's gotten pretty good at shitting so it doesn't run down his leg. O, I used a long handled dish mop and a bucket of warm water to wash his butt if necessary before putting his tail back in, usually it isn't.

Yeah, well I like hairy dogs so I just keep his head clipped short but don't shave anything except his cock and balls. Yeah I play with them everyday; he gets to cum maybe once a month humping my leg. I like keeping him horny. He sleeps in a dog kennel, inside in the mudroom during the winter and out on the porch once it got warm enough. Yeah he comes in the house once in a while, but not too often until it gets cold out. When I'm out here with him I let him run free. Well, not really free - I use this remote controlled electric collar on his balls to keep him in line. When he's out of sight or ignoring me I just push this button here and watch him jump. It's also handy for encouraging him with those weights. We spend about a couple of hours a day working out together. I set goals for him (number of sit-ups or pushups or weight pressed) and if he can't quite meet them the electric collar on his cock is an incentive. You know that gadget is really handy. When I set it low it just tingles. He's learned a whole routine. Want to see it? Watch - one buzz gets his attention "Right boy!" Two buzzes and he comes. Watch what happens with three - that's right, he freezes in place like a pointer. "Very good, boy!" Two short and a long, see he rolls over on his back, isn't he cute, paws up, legs wide open. Usually I play with his balls in this position. There's a lot more he can do. "Come on boy come get your treat."

Oh you're wondering about his paws. The canvas ones aren't as fancy as leather ones, but he gets them muddy and I can just wash them off and let them dry without ruining them. About the only time they come off is to trim his nails and to use the weights. And food? Oh I feed him regular people food... I just chop it up and mush it all together so it looks like dog food. In the morning he sometimes gets a bowl of dry cereal with piss instead of milk - yeah I really get into piss. He drinks all of mine, and anyone else's who's visiting as well. Oh I guess my real perversity is that since his second day here he hasn't had a meal that wasn't mixed with my piss. Don't know if he likes it, but he really doesn't have much of a say in the matter does he. Ha ha.

So anymore questions, no? Oh you need to take off? Need to piss before you go? Okay. "Bowzer, get over here. Time for a drink."

A LUCKY PUP

By goodpup

Last night, tied up, the poetry of restraint, manacled to the chair, hooded, alone, the sound of His truck pulling out of the drive, and me, left there, powerless, in the dark, my balls weighted. Scared.

"Sir? Sir? Please Sir, i will be good Sir, i will obey You Sir. Please?"

No answer. Alone. Panic rises, then sinks, as calm sets in, deep certain calm, entry into sub-space. Thank you Sir. Time passes, but soon becomes meaningless. The constant pull on my balls becomes more obvious, pushing its way into my brain. Pain. Must be borne, nothing else to do with it. Feel the pain, turn it into pleasure. That's my role. At last, i hear the truck pull back into the drive. i knew He would return. Overjoyed, i get ready to greet my Master with the respect He deserves.

Later, gagged, dribbling, tits clamped hard, begging on my knees like a pup, paws in front. No response through the gag possible, just muffled cries. The hood is still on, but the blindfold has been removed.

"Is that good eh pup?" he asks as the pain shoots through my tits, a bright red rose of agony each one.

"You like that huh?"
"NO!" i try and shout, but nothing comes out, all i can do is go Humph and whine, in agony.

"Whining in pleasure huh pup? Good pup, your Master will give you some more now."

Another weight is added to my balls, dragging them harder through the ball separator. My body is begging for release, but i can't say anything. The gag makes me dribble more as i try and beg for mercy through it. i

5

look at him and roll my eyes, whimpering.

"Good pup, that's right, you like it when your Master plays with you don't you pup. If you're real good you might get a bone later."

He leaned over and ruffled my hair, then with is other hand turned the titclamps even tighter. The weights hanging from my balls are swinging back and forward, and fuck do they hurt.

The pain is building, taking over my body, when my mind clicks, switches into sub-space where it wants to be. And then the pain is fine. Still there, but my offering to my Master. My pain is His pleasure, and that gives me pleasure, so my pain is good. Calm, ecstasy. He senses the change in me, the quiet and acceptance. He knows what He has done. He gets up, and moves behind me. I hear His black leather bag unzip and then He takes something out of it. He returns in front of me, still begging like a pup up on my hind legs, front paws out, clamps tight on my tits, balls hanging painfully low. He puts His arms under my elbows and raises me to my feet. "Good pup, good boy, you're being a good little pup now for me aren't you?"

Filled with gratitude and respect I look up at His face briefly, and then return my gaze to His feet where it belongs. He now has a flogger attached to His belt. i cringe, whimper at the sight of it. Heavy black leather tails.

"For you boy, for being a good pup tonight," he tells me as he fastens my manacles to the hooks in the door frame. Stretched out now, and above me, my arms increase the pressure on the clamps to a new explosion of pain. I whimper and whine, start to writhe.

"Steady boy," he says, levelly, calmly, but with that tone of command that i know means things will get worse if i misbehave.

He kneels, the only time He ever does in front of me, to fasten my ankles to the bottom of the door frame, then steps back and lights a cigarette.

"Good boy, I like you like that boy. You just wait there while I have a beer and a smoke." He comes up behind me and whispers in my ear, harshly, "I want you to think how lucky you are, just keep telling yourself how lucky you are that I am here doing this to you, you scum sucking dogboy slave!"

With that, He clipped the blindfold back over my eyes and i heard the door behind me close as He left me, and i did as i was instructed.

After a while my body aches so much from the pain, the tits and the ball-weights, and i can hardly move because of the manacles. He comes up behind me and i can feel his dick pressing into my arse through his leather pants, i feel so happy that He is back again, and so scared as well. He puts his arms around me, so strong and warm. This makes me feel so good. Then He works my tits. Hard. From behind the gag I am dribbling a torrent, i am trying to beg him to stop, trying, but the only noises i can make are muffled howls.

"Good boy, that's right, say thank you pup. I understand pup, you're very happy now."

The pain is amazing, clean and hot. He stops and pulls the blindfold from the hood again, and then suddenly the lashes of the flogger are in front of my face. He pushes them against my saliva wet gagged mouth.

"Kiss the whip boy. You know you need it, kiss it. You know you like it. and i know i don't care if you do or not, I like it."

Then He steps back, and my terror mounts. My dick is rock hard in front of me now. Totally powerless, immobilized, i hear the swish of the tails, and then feel the sting as they land. Hard. Hot. Pains, spreading through my butt, good and bad at the same time, again and again, more heat, more pain, getting better. My Master is right. i do need this, i do want it. I am lucky He is concerned enough with a mangy stray pup like me to train me. The joy of being owned and trained acts like alchemy on the pain, and my mind soars free as the lash falls again and again, on my butt and my back.

Drool is hanging from my mouth in strings, my tits are on fire, my balls are screaming with agony and yet i feel free and happy. i lose count of the blows; just sink into the rhythmic tide of their intensity, like waves crashing over me, washing me. My back and arse feel like they are a live, pulsing bed of red-hot light. So good. My arsehole is wet and begging to be fucked. my entire body has been turned into a series of over worked nerves. Then the beating stops, and i feel His dick again, as He pushes into me, pushes His cock up my arse, pushing my body in its restraints, i squeeze His dick as He fills my arse, fucking me harder and deeper.

"Good pup, good boy, see, be good and you get a bone. You're a lucky pup aren't you?"

And i know that i am.

COLLARD AT THE DOG POUND

by Christopher Pierce

I didn't expect to get claimed and collared by a Master that night, but I did.

I certainly didn't expect to get pumped full of piss and cum in a back room, but that's exactly what happened.

I definitely never thought I'd be carried out of a bar by the hottest man there, but I did that night.

Lots of boys got collared and claimed at the Dog Pound, everyone knew that. I just never thought I'd be lucky enough to have it happen to me.

The Dog Pound was the most popular bar in town, always packed full of the hottest leathermen you could ask for. Every night you could feast your eyes on an incredible assortment of male flesh. The place was bursting at the seams with enough sights, smells and tastes to fill my dreams for months at a time.

Thick clouds of tobacco smoke that were laced with the odors of beer and sweat. Shiny black boots that made you want to drop to your knees and worship them right then and there. Muscles stretching the fabric of t-shirts 'til it ripped. Crotches plump and full, the delicious hardness beneath enough to drive you mad with desire. And everywhere, everywhere was leather.

Leather chaps parting to reveal perfect round ass-cheeks. Leather vests with stains so dark you wonder if they're sweat, cum or blood. Leather collars encircling the necks of lucky slaves already claimed as property.

I went to the Dog Pound fairly often, always thrilling to the sight of Masters choosing boys to claim and keep. It was easy to tell the ones who were serious, apart from the others. Lots of men just came to the Dog Pound to cruise and soak up the atmosphere.

But the real crowd, the crowd the place was famous for, was the hard-core SM/BD Master/slave crowd. Those were men who took the life seriously, who saw leather as a lifestyle, not just something to wear on Saturday nights.

You could always tell the hard-core Masters from the dress-ups. It was hard to explain, but it was like an attitude, a way of carrying himself, that tipped you off. It was in the way a biker cap was tilted back on a head, the way a pair of eyes smoked when they saw a choice piece of meat, the way a hand thoughtfully stroked a newly grown mustache or goatee.

Whatever it was, it kept me up night after night, dreaming and hoping and longing for a day when I would be ready to be claimed by a real man and taken home as his property.

The boys, the ones who thought they were hot enough to be claimed, were easy to tell from the others. An unwritten law decreed that boys who wanted to be claimed wore a plain black armband, on their right arm of course, as the signal to the Masters that they thought they made the grade.

Whether they did or not, of course, was up to the Masters.

That was the terrifying part. I had seen many boys who thought they were ready for real slavery humiliated in front of the entire crowd, scorned and spit upon and sent home alone when they were found unsuitable. As much as I wanted to be owned, the fear of being disgraced like that was even more powerful. Boys deemed unworthy never showed their butts or faces in the Dog Pound again.

The nightly drama went on and on, as savage and primitive in its own way as the spectacles enjoyed by the Greeks and Romans. There was something mystical and powerful in it, like watching an age-old rite enacted over and over again.

The Masters searched and hunted, their focus of attention always the same: the corner of the room designated for those who wanted to be claimed.

There, under a sign that read "LOST DOGS", the boys stood. Some were frightened, others proud and arrogant. Sometimes they were as far away from each other as they could be, other times huddled together like the pack of scared dogs they were. The boys preened and strutted in front of the Masters like wild birds showing off exotic plumage, each one's mind burning with the singular desire to catch a Master's fancy and to be taken to the back room of the bar.

That was where the Masters determined if boys were truly ready or not. That was where the testing happened. Few men knew for sure what was back there, and you didn't know what to believe.

There were rumors that the room was a horrific dungeon, filled with devices of unspeakable torture. Boys that failed the tests performed in that room, were lower than dog shit.

To present yourself as ready, when it was not true, was the worst crime a boy could commit, and he was never allowed back again.

The boys that passed the test were the envy of all the others. Pleasing a Master and being claimed by him was the goal of every one of them, but few accomplished it. There was some secret to the testing that only a small number of boys seemed to grasp.

The ultimate dream of course, beyond being claimed, was to have a Master buy something for you at the in-bar store. It was a tiny boutique that sold everything a Master could want for his new dog: collars, leashes, dog bowls, bondage equipment...

The happiest boys in the world were the ones who were claimed and then taken to the store to have something bought for them. When their Masters led them out, on leashes, and headed for the exit, that were practically barking for joy.

The other boys would howl and whine in sympathy, and go back to trying to find a Master of their own.

But the fear of the testing kept many from entering the lost dogs corner. What actually happened during the testing was not discussed. No boy who had ever gone through it would talk about it, and the Masters were distant and unapproachable. It was a private thing, whatever it was that went on in the shadowy dark of the back room at the Dog Pound.

I never dreamed I would experience it myself.

Morbidly shy, I was a loner that kept to myself. A very wise Master, a friend of a friend, who I had learned a lot from, had trained me as a slave. He had been happy to train me, but already had a stable of slaves so he couldn't keep me for his own.

I knew I needed to be owned by a man, a real Master, but something prevented me from looking in the usual places. No computer bulletin boards or personal ads for me. It had to be in person, it had to be physical. A few years before I had had my tarot cards done and the reader told me that without a doubt, the man I was going to spend my life with would come to me, not the other way around.

Telling myself I wouldn't be following the vision of the cards if I put on an armband and strutted my stuff, I had a convenient excuse not to join the other boys. But it was only partly true. The other part was that I was scared to death of failing the test and being humiliated in front of all those men.

So I kept a low profile at the Dog Pound, trying to blend in as much as possible. I hung out at the back wall, as far away from the Lost Dogs corner and the Masters perusing it as possible. Watching in silence, I thought I was invisible.

You can imagine my surprise that night I was singled out and spoken to.

"You." The voice was somehow as clear as a bell despite the raucous noise of the bar. It was deep, seeming to rumble the floorboards like some kind of stereo speaker test. I wondered who on earth was lucky enough, or unfortunate enough, to be called by that voice.

That was when the crowd parted. I couldn't believe my eyes as I watched the men all around me back away and a passageway open up that crossed the whole length of the place. At one end was me, at the other was a man - a man that was unmistakably the owner of that voice.

"You." he said again, and the crowd quieted down, their eyes moving back and forth between him and me.

I stared at the man in disbelief.

He was tall, over six feet. His face was strong, masculine. His body was sturdy and heavy - mostly muscle. In contrast to the absurdly elaborate costumes most of the men were wearing, he had adorned himself simply: black leather jacket, white t-shirt, blue jeans and work boots. His hair was plain brown, short like his beard. Far from the most good-looking of the Masters, he was definitely the most striking. Something about him demanded respect and got it, from Masters and slaves alike.

And he was talking to me.

Pain in my jeans snapped me out of my trance. My cock had hardened up in my snugly-fitting underwear and now was bending painfully. I adjusted myself, feeling my ears turn red at the playful laughter of the crowd.

Was he really looking at me? Knowing what I looked like - and him short close-cropped blond hair, nice face, decent body - I didn't see how I could have drawn his attention among all these men. I was handsome, but nothing compared to the show dogs in the corner that even now were glaring unhappily at me, their spotlight stolen.

But I didn't want their spotlight. I just wanted to watch unnoticed.

"I'm not going to say it again." the man said.

Watching unnoticed was no longer an option.

"You got a voice, boy?" he said, more loudly this time.

Etiquette and manners slammed back into me all at once.

"Yes, Sir!" I said, bowing my head, "I'm sorry, Sir."

"That's better. Come here."

As if in a dream, I crossed the room through the corridor of men. Keeping my eyes on the floor, I could feel a hundred eyes probing me, in lust, jealousy, approval - so many emotions were competing. But I knew I had the luxury of only one emotion: obedience. My cock was demanding attention, but there was no time for that.

I stood before the man, my head still bowed.

"What do they call you, boy?" he said, more softly. Close up, his voice took on even more power, a bass tremor that seemed to enter my body and make it tremble from within.

"Billy, Sir." I said.

"I'm Kirk, but you'll call me Sir. Is that clear?"

"Sir, yes, Sir!" I said.

"No boy calls me Master unless he earns it."

"Yes, Sir, I understand, Sir."

In his presence my cock firmed up even more, blood rushing into it as if the man's mere proximity was causing actual chemical changes in my body.

This was without a doubt the most powerful Master I had ever seen, much less been addressed by.

"Are you presently owned by anyone, Billy?" he asked.

"Sir, no, Sir." I said. "But Sir..."

"Yes, boy?"

"Why...me? There are so many hot boys over in that corner dying to get claimed..." He interrupted me.

"I don't want a dog that would parade himself around in that manner. In my opinion, that's behavior unbecoming of a boy."

"Then why come here, Sir?" I asked. "This place is famous for..." Again he cut me off.

"I know what it's famous for, boy. I come here hoping to find a boy that's right for me. A boy that's interested in serving and belonging to a man, not strutting up and down like a goddamn belle of the ball."

He looked at me hard, as if trying to decide if he had made a mistake picking me or not. I lowered my head even more, trying to show him I was not belligerent, just curious.

"You got a problem with that?" he said suddenly.

"Sir, no, Sir!" I answered instantly.

"Glad to hear it. Now, let's not waste any more time. You might be the dog I've been looking for, Billy. I'm interested in finding out. Are you?"

I couldn't believe my ears, but wasn't stupid enough to say so.

"Oh, yes, thank you Sir!"

Kirk smiled and put one hand on the back of my neck. To actually have him touch me, to have him take me into his control, was intoxicating. His hand was firm and steady on my neck. I tried to keep my balance as he led me from the brightly lit main area to the door that led to the back room, the place of testing.

The crowd murmured in approval and awe as we walked through the door and out of sight. We walked through several twists and turns in the dark hallway, until we came to a large empty room. The only light was a few candles here and there.

"Surprised, boy?" Kirk said.

"A little, Sir." The thought of telling this man anything but the truth never occurred to me.

"You were expecting a dungeon, right? A big playroom with lots of slings and cages and bondage equipment."

"Yes, Sir."

"You're surprised, but are you disappointed?" he asked. I turned to look up at him for the first time.

"No, Sir."

He smiled again and my heart soared.

"Good boy." he said. "Toys and dungeons are all well and good, but if a Master can't dominate a boy with just himself, then he's no Master."

"What do you mean, Sir?" I asked.

"Do you know why so few boys are actually claimed? Because they expect this room to be the big dungeon of their dreams, and when they're actually brought here, they're disappointed and show themselves unworthy."

"Unworthy, Sir?"

The flickering light of the candles made him look eerie and magical, like a medieval sorcerer sharing secret knowledge with an apprentice.

"Yes. Their disappointment shows that what they're after is a hot scene, not to be an owned piece of property. They want to get worked over with lots of toys and equipment, not to just serve a man however he wants to be served."

He looked at me sternly.

"They're not real slaves, they're selfish bottoms unfit to be claimed. But I think you're a real slave."

"Thank you, Sir!" I said.

"We're very much alike, Billy. Look at how we dress. Plain, functional, clothes to cover our bodies and keep them warm. Look how we act. Off to the side, away from the spotlight, never drawing attention to ourselves."

"I've never seen you here before, Sir." I said, and he laughed.

"I've been here every night since the Dog Pound opened, boy. But few see me. I don't like a lot of attention. I only show myself if I think there's a chance I've found a real slave, which has happened very few times."

I dropped to my knees and bowed my head, my cock a jutting spike in my pants.

"Oh please, Sir, how can I prove it to you? What test can I take to show you I'm a true slave?"

I heard the clinking of his belt being unfastened and knew that the moment of truth had come at last. It looked like it was not going to be the test that the boys whispered and wondered about. It would not be a test of endurance, to see how much torture a boy could take. It would be nothing as obvious and vulgar as that.

It would simply be a test to see if I could serve and please this man well enough for him to want to claim me.

Kirk's dick came out from the slit of his jeans' fly and it was beautiful to see - Big, uncut, veiny, hard as a rock. I lunged forward with animal violence, taking it into my mouth like a starving man who has finally found food.

It was heaven. His cock was right at home inside me, leaking pre-cum out as I stroked and caressed it with my tongue. Kirk grunted in satisfaction and put his hands on my head to anchor me in place.

He started fucking my face, plunging his boner in and out of my mouth.

"Yeah, boy," he said. "You're just here to be used. I'm going to use all your holes the same way...your mouth, your ass, it's all the same to me, just holes to fuck."

My own dick was begging for attention now. I could almost feel the stain of pre-cum that was no doubt seeping through the crotch of my jeans. But I knew that my hands belonged behind my back, that to do anything other than what was ordered of me would be a monumental mistake.

Without warning, totally unexpected, my time had come. My test was now, and I was going to do everything I could to pass.

Kirk was pounding me so hard I almost couldn't breathe. The blood-engorged club in my mouth slammed against the back of my throat over and over again.

"That's it." he said. "Take it boy, that's all you're here for. Just to take my dick wherever I want to put it. You're here just to serve and please me, that's all you're good for."

Bile was rising in my gut. I gagged and choked, trying to signal Kirk that I was having trouble.

"I don't care if you're going to throw up, slave. It feels good on my cock. If you throw up, you'll just get down there and lick it back up until the floor is nice and clean like it was when you came in here."

I knew there was no use in trying to resist him. Resigning myself to letting whatever happened occur without fighting, my mind relaxed. Miraculously, my stomach calmed down and the puking feeling disappeared. I was there just to serve, to take his dick and make him feel good.

Then he pushed in as far as he could go. His boner filled my whole mouth. My nostrils flared to take in the oxygen I needed. But his hand clamped down on my nose, pinching it and cutting off all air. I was plugged up completely and panic exploded in my brain.

"You'll breathe when I let you, boy." Kirk said.

Fear tried to get a foot-hold in me but I fought it down. My hands wanted to push him away, but I controlled myself and kept them behind my back. I tried to stay calm as Kirk started counting slowly.

"1...2...3...4...5...6...7...8...9...10."

He released me, letting my nose go and pulling out of my mouth. I sucked in as much air as I could, gasping and panting.

"Good boy," he said. "Now get on your hands and knees like the dog you are."

Still trying to recover from the breath control, I maneuvered onto my hands and knees with my butt in the air. He kneeled down behind me, his hands snaking around my waist to unfasten my pants and yank them down. He seized my underwear and ripped it off of me, tearing it to shreds.

My cock sprang out into the air, released at last. Its head shimmered with pre-cum in the candlelight.

Kirk's enormous weight settled on me from behind. I didn't know how I could support him and take his dick up my ass at the same time, but I'd do it somehow. This test had to be passed, no matter what.

"You want to be my dog, Billy?" he asked.

"Oh, yes, yes Sir!" I said.

His cock was nosing around my butt hole. I heard the sound of plastic and latex and knew he was sliding a condom over his big meat. He hocked up some spit and let it fall, then used to it to slime up his cock and get it ready for entry.

My muscles were tense with nervousness and excitement. I tried to relax so that it wouldn't be too painful, but it was too late. Kirk plunged his huge dick into my asshole, breaking through the sphincter ring like it was nothing. I screamed like a virgin getting his cherry popped

"Yeah, howl like a good dog, boy, howl for me..."

White-hot fire was burning my brain as I forced myself to stand still. I longed to crawl forward, to force him out of me, but I steeled my arms and legs and stood my ground. How could I back out now when he seemed to be pleased with me? I didn't know how it was possible to be in such pain and such pleasure at the same time.

But there I was, on my hands and knees getting my ass plowed on the floor of the Dog Pound's back room. It was the last thing in the world I expected to happen, yet here it was: my chance to be claimed once and for all by a real Master had come.

But only if I could prove I was a real slave.

I pushed my ass backwards, engulfing his cock even further inside me. Kirk exhaled loudly and groaned in pleasure.

"Yeah, push back, dog, push your slave ass back on my big dick..."

"Yes, Sir!" I gasped. It felt like my spine was going to snap under the strain of the huge man laying on top of me. The fire in my head burned hotter as he started pile-driving me. In and out of me his cock surged, its forward-backward motion as precise and insistent as an oil well's.

I tried to concentrate, as difficult as it was. My knees were getting scraped raw through my jeans on the rough floor. Somehow I found a secret place in my mind, a place where everything was calm.

It was a place of utter submission, where all my needs and desires fell away to leave one and one alone: the desire to serve.

My job, my purpose, my whole reason for being crystallized in that moment. I was here just to serve this man. That was all. There was room for nothing else in my existence.

Just to serve.

"Yeah, dog boy, your ass is so fucking hot...I'm going to cum..."

He thrust into me harder than ever before, seeming to force his dick up past my stomach into my guts. He reamed me wide open; making it feel like my whole body was splitting in two. I screamed again, and this time my cry was joined by the man above me.

His cock jerked like a machine-gun, shooting off blast after blast inside me. Kirk's whole body shook, quivering and trembling as if from an internal earthquake.

"Good dog..." he murmured in my ear. "Good dog..."

Despite the pain in my arms, legs and ass, I felt elation at his approval. I was pleasing him! Maybe I would pass the test!

But it wasn't over yet.

He pulled out of me and it felt like he was taking my whole insides with him. With his cock gone I felt empty and naked. But there was no time to dwell on that, because he walked around to stand in front of me again.

Kirk was holding the condom in his hand, its end full and plump with his jizz. He suddenly dumped it out onto me, the cum splashing onto my chest and dripping down into my crotch. His big hands came forward, rubbing it into the fabric of my shirt, into my skin. Its warm stickiness felt magical on my body, like some kind of enchanted potion or salve.

"Thank you, Sir..." I moaned.

"What do you want, dog boy?" he asked.

"Just to serve you, Sir." I said. "Just to serve you."

He stood over me, the candlelight making his shadow flicker and sway on the walls. His features and the details of his body were lost in the dark, making him indistinct but definitely a figure of male virility. The man above me could have been an ancient cave man, a Roman gladiator, a warrior from the future; it didn't matter.

All that mattered, more than anything in the world, was that I serve and please him and pass his test.

"Open your mouth, dog slave," he said, and I obediently did so. "Clean my cock," he said as he stepped forward.

His dick felt wonderful in my mouth, its delicious softness full and ecstatic on my tongue. I caressed and massaged it as if it were a delicate porcelain object, more priceless and valuable than any treasure in the world.

"Now," Kirk said. "Jerk yourself off."

Disbelief and joy flooded my brain. My hand grabbed my cock and started pumping it up and down. Jacking myself had never felt so sweet.

I wanted to thank him so badly, but my mouth was stuffed full of cock so there was no chance of that. The intensity of all that happened was like a wave that was washing over me, filling me with ecstasy I had never known before.

All I wanted to do was serve this man.

And right now it served him to jerk myself off.

"What a good boy," I heard him say. "What a good dog."

And a flood of piss surged out of his flaccid cock into my mouth and down my gullet. I coughed and slobbered, trying not to let any of the precious fluid hit the floor. It was unbelievable to be filled by his warmth, to take something of his directly from his body into my own.

I was a total boy, a total dog...a total dog slave.

"Cum for me, dog slave!" Kirk said, and I did.

Spunk splattered up out of me and hit my chin. The pleasure that blossomed inside me was hotter than I'd ever felt before, and it was eclipsed by my surprise at my own ability. I had never shot this hard or this far before. The orgasm roared through me, as Kirk continued pissing down my throat.

My brain almost exploded with the overwhelming sensations flooding through me...the feel of his cock in my mouth, the bitter warmth of his piss flowing into me, the white-hot charge of my hand around my own dick, the rainbow firestorm of my own cumming...

The last drops of his urine dribbled out of his dick and he backed away. I fell forward onto the floor, prostrate at his feet.

"Thank you, Sir..." I moaned with my last bit of strength. "Thank you for the privilege of serving you."

Exhausted, I would have passed out had the events about to take place not stunned me back to consciousness.

"You've served me well, Billy," he said. "I was right about you. You're not like those other boys out there. You don't want to primp and preen in front of a bunch of men. You just want to serve a man with your whole body, mind and soul, and be his property forever."

"Yes, Sir." I whispered.

"I've been waiting a long time for this moment."

I hoped he was going to say that I passed the test, but he didn't. Glancing up, I saw that he had kneeled down and was just looking at me, a tiny smile on his face.

"If you've been here every night since the bar opened, it must have been a very long time, Sir," I said, desperate to say something, anything to fill the yawning silence of his stare.

"Yes, it has." he said. "But trying to find a boy of my own isn't the only reason I'm here so much. I also need to keep an eye on the place, make sure it's running well, that the customers are happy."

That went right over my head. I stared at Kirk in confusion.

"I...don't understand, Sir."

"I own the Dog Pound, Billy." he said simply.

"But, but if you own it," I said. "Why do you let all those men parade around? Why the Lost Dogs corner? You said you hated all that stuff..."

"I do," he said. "But it's good for business. It brings people in. I figured if I set the bait, the Masters and the boys would come. If I made this the hottest leather bar in town, eventually the boy I wanted would come...and then I would go to him, and test him, and make him mine."

And then I would go to him...I thought. Just like the tarot cards said would happen...I didn't go to him, he came to me by singling me out among all the boys...

"Wait," I said, trying to wrap my mind around all that had happened. "You mean you opened this bar just to find a slave for yourself..."

"Yes. Don't get me wrong, Billy. It's fun owning a bar and everything, but I don't need to. I've got more money than I know what to do with. I knew the boy I wanted couldn't be bought."

I lowered my head.

"I'm sure he'll be a very lucky boy." I said dejectedly.

Kirk threw back his head and started laughing. Great peals of mirth spilled out of him, so loud I was sure the men in the bar could hear him. It made me mad to be made fun of that way, especially after I had tried so hard to please him. I was about to ask him to stop when he spoke again.

"It's you, Billy."

"What, Sir?" I said dumbly. He rose to his feet and pulled me up with him. Instinctively I pulled my jeans up and fastened them tight again. Staring into Kirk's eyes, I tried desperately to understand what he was saying.

"It's you." he said again. "You're the boy I've been looking for all these years. You're the one."

"Did I..." I started, but the words wouldn't come out.

"Yes," he said, nodding. "You passed the test."

The smile that lit up my face must have been bright enough to fill the whole room, and I started babbling like an idiot.

"Oh, thank you, Sir! It was so hard sometimes, but I just kept focusing on serving and pleasing you and not thinking about anything else..."

He put his hand over my mouth and my monologue trailed off.

"That wasn't the test." he said. "You had passed the test before I even fucked your face."

This piece of information was almost too much for me to handle.

"Please explain, Sir..." I said.

"When we first came in this room, and you said you weren't disappointed that it was just a room, not a dungeon, I knew everything I needed to know about you."

My heart was full, like I had stumbled onto something wondrous and beautiful without even trying to. But it was something I didn't understand.

"You're the first that ever answered that you weren't disappointed." Kirk said. "I knew that you were there to serve, not be a pushy boy that wanted to top from the bottom up. I knew you were a true slave, a real dog slave."

Without thinking, I rushed forward and hugged him. The joy I felt was indescribable.

"Thank you, Sir, oh thank you, Sir!" I cried as I leaned my head on his chest.

His arms came around me and it was like paradise.

Then I felt him get something out of his pocket. I almost fell to his feet again as I felt a sensation I always wanted but never hoped for: the sensation of a leather collar being slipped around my neck and the sound of it being locked into place.

"Thank you, Sir."

"Let's get out of here." he said, and together we walked back through the twisting hallway to the door that led to the bar. It was like walking on air.

The light of the main room blinded me as we stepped through the door. There was an audible gasp of delight as the crowd saw the collar around my neck.

Kirk put his hand on my shoulder and pushed me down onto my knees. A hush fell over the crowd and they seemed to hold their breath in anticipation.

"Billy." Kirk said in that voice that had shook me to my core.

"Yes, Sir?" I said obediently. The room was silent, our voices clear and plain.

"From now on you will call me Master."

"Yes, Sir. Thank you, Sir." I said.

The crowd cheered, roaring like a winning team's fans. All around us the men clinked their beer bottles together in tribute to us, clapped Kirk on the back and shook his hand, some of them petting me, and all of them congratulating us.

After a few minutes I was getting very tired, swaying back and forth on my bended knees. The spectacle of the night was overwhelming me, and I couldn't deal with much more. I was dying of happiness at being claimed at last.

My Master sensed this and got me to my feet. Then, without a moment's hesitation he scooped me up in his arms and hoisted me over his shoulder like a sack of potatoes.

"C'mon, dog boy," he said. "Time to take you to your new home."

The crowd went wild again and watched as my Master carried me to the in-bar store.

I heard him talk to the boy behind the counter. He grinned at the sight of this incredibly hot man with a boy slung over his shoulder and reached back to get what my Master asked for. Kirk acted as if I was no more a burden to him than if he had his jacket over his shoulder. I was just one more thing that belonged to him, and he was carrying it just like he would anything else.

He took what the boy handed him with the hand that wasn't holding me in place, and then let it drop to his side. From where I was hanging I could see what it was...a brand new shiny black dog bowl.

I was floating on a cloud.

My new Master waved good-bye to his friends and employees and took me, his new property, out the door. Fresh night air greeted us as he carried me out into the parking lot, where his truck was waiting for us.

DEVIL DOG PUPS

By PFC-USMC Devil Dawg

I hate to admit it, but I must consider myself and all the other hot young jarheads along with me "young pups." It's like being a Marine puppy. See, boots (Marines who haven't reached the two year mark yet) are inexperienced in many ways. To me, it isn't until you reach Sergeant or above that you start really blossoming as a Marine, or it's not until you've seen combat. I just think that all Privates and PFCs and even Lance Corporals are the Corps "puppies". I have a raunchier term for all the Marines between the ages of 17 or 18 through 22. I call 'em "young guts" Go figure. Just picture a hot young jarhead, all young and inexperienced. Thinks he knows the world, but doesn't know shit.

Picture that same jarhead down on his knees, sucking your cock. Pounding his fucking head in with your much larger, experienced, cock. Imagine how it must feel to have his young face battered by your muscular stomach. How it must feel for him. All his whimpers. All his moans. He looks up at you with his beautiful blue boy eyes. All you seen in his eyes is the innocence that's being pounded out of him with each fuck thrust. He's a good boy though. He can take it. He's been to Parris Island for boot camp. He grew up in the South, eatin' meat n' potatoes. He was the high school jock. Star football player, now he's down on his knees in the head. With your Sergeant cock pounding his face in. You decide to pull out, and saliva and pre-cum drip from your cock to his young chin. You take the sweet moment to watch as it slowly oozes down his chin and neck, all the way down.

He's all hot n' sweaty now, and soiled by your pre-cum. He wants it bad; he wants it up the ass. He begs for it. He wants it so fucking bad. He gives you that ready look, and you order him to get on his back on the deck. The bathroom floor. You pull his legs up on your shoulders and you aim your cock at his young innocent Marine hole. You force feed your prick into him and you get off on his loud cry of pain, and you tell him to suck it the fuck up. Suck it up. Look at you now, you have this hot little young gut on his back on the deck and you're beginning to pound every last bit of boyness out of him, for you are turning him into a true Marine. Manhood comes with pain, it's part of the territory.

You begin to fuck him hard, he whimpers young devil dawg pup whimpers, and he squirms while you invade him. His young gut is hot and wet and ready. You fuck him and he looks up at you, occasionally rolling his beautiful boy blue eyes back into his little Marine head. You keep fucking him. Buckin' the boy. You are getting off like a mad dawg at this point. You're teaching him what manhood is all about. Ahhh, oh yeah, fuck me, ahhh, yeah, give it to me Sergeant, he screams, he manages to keep his bearing and respect for you while you're tearing the innocence out of him. Oh yeah, ahh fuck yeah, fuck that goddamn ass sergeant, oh fuck ahhh unhhh, he cries. By now you are ready to cum, you don't even warn him, and it catches him off guard.

You let lose with jet after forceful jet of hot man cum, Marine cum, shoots its way all through his young pup guts. Loads and loads of juicy fuck cream blast his insides. He whimpers at it. He just lies there, battered and abused, but made a man. He's at the beginning stages of manhood now, and although he has a lot to learn, he's just learned the most important part of being a man and being a Marine......

DOGSLAVE

by Cager

Part I

It started as a fantasy. i had always had a foot in both the standard gay culture and another in the SM culture, content to dabble in one or the other when it suited me; but as time went on i found myself less and less drawn to the 'vanilla' side of gay sex and more and more to the sm. Even here i had problems because any guy i chose to go off with always seemed to be into something in a big way that i myself was not. i tried to get into it, whatever it was, simply to learn - i wanted to learn about myself, to explore those aspects of myself that i knew were hidden from me by all the distractions of everyday life, of being obliged to go about everyday mundane business.

i started out by defining myself as passive. Those were the earliest days and then there was little difference between the vanilla and SM worlds i moved between. 'S&M' sex to me was being fucked by a guy in a leather jacket. Then that wasn't enough and i started to become choosy. Now i would only go with men in full leather, or full uniform, and i knew that i did not want to be solely passive but also submissive.

As a submissive i wanted to be controlled and ordered about - in a friendly kind of way; this was all just acting. i didn't get off on pain but went along with it when it seemed it might take me lower and lower to the place where my submissiveness lay. i also discovered that if i got down deep enough then i gladly accepted punishment - that is, not pain for pain's sake but pain with a purpose.

Then i called myself a slave - acting again and becoming good at the part. i began to see that my submission deepened when it was accompanied by verbal abuse. i began to get into the idea of humiliation and degradation and these led me to the heart of the matter where all these things met.

One day i knew, with blinding certainty, that even life as a slave would not satisfy my needs. i needed to go lower still, down; right down to the centre of my submission and it was there that i recognized myself as a dog. Yes, only as a dog could all my needs be met - to be humiliated, to be degraded, to be beaten for infractions of rules, to obey, to be trained, to be controlled, to be owned.

It had been a long journey to this point but this was only a beginning. Accepting in myself that i was a dog was one thing, but how to do something about it? i needed a trainer, a dog handler, someone who was interested in treating me as sub-human, an animal, a dog. i tried placing an ad in a gay contact magazine but had no success. i went to leather clubs wearing a dog collar with a leash hanging from it and had a few scenes as a result after i had explained to the Master that i was looking for a dog scene and not just a slave scene. But the sessions never lasted long and the Master would see it as just a bit of fantasy, fine for a few minutes but no more, and go back to more standard SM practices.

my trainer was a recommendation. The SM scene was small enough even in a large city for a kind of informal club to evolve where people came to know other people's particular needs and obsessions. So I heard about him on the grapevine, made inquiries and then made contact by phone. we discussed it in depth, looking at it from every point of view we could think of and now i was going for my first training session to become the dog that i knew i really was.

The discussions were extensive because the Master would not waste his time on a human who just jerked off over the idea of something slightly different. He wanted to know my seriousness, my commitment, my potential to become a dog, a dogslave, devoted to my Master, always obedient, always submissive, just a dog, an animal that would lose its human side, would start to think like a dog and so behave naturally like a dog. We discussed my life style and schedule and i gave him a detailed account of my daily movements. He proposed a contract. If i accepted it then i would have to stand by it and act according to it. First would come my induction, followed by a week of intensive training; then i would be free to leave but would remain on call as his dog; he could phone me at any time of the day or night and i would instantly have to revert to dog mode - it might be that my training would continue over the phone or i might have to drop everything and report to him as his dog. He promised me that, if i accepted this contract, i would have to lose human behavior patterns, human speech, and bark and growl and whine and pant as a dog. He promised me that, after my initial training, i would be so programmed that this would come entirely naturally no matter what i might be doing at the time he called. my first training session would be the handshake on the contract for there would be a ceremony in which i would be formally inducted as a dogslave and after that there would be no going back. He questioned me as to my present level of experience and said it would soon be tested.

The Master sounded ideal. He had been a dog handler in the forces, he bred Rottweilers so there was nothing he did not know about training canines, plus he had all the amenities - collars, chains, and cages to train these animals. i was going to join them as a dogslave. The Master's military background gave him an obsession with discipline and obedience and he knew he had the authority, the manner, the attitude, the bearing, to carry it out.

my instructions had been explicit. i would find the door of the Master's house ajar. i would step into the hall, close the door and immediately fall to my knees. i would remain on my knees after that and would never stand up in the presence of the Master; the Master would in fact never see me except as a dog. This meant that the Master, never having seen me as a human, would see me only as a dog and treat me like one accordingly. On my knees, i was then to strip and put all my human clothes in a bag and leave it by the door. Then i would place the large dog collar around my neck, buckle on the muzzle, and attach the chain leash to the dog collar. On all fours i would crawl along the corridor, go down stairs into the cellar where i would find a dog cage. i would crawl into it, chain myself to the bars of the cage, slam the door of the cage and lock the padlock and then wait. While i was waiting i was to think only as a dog, telling myself over and over and over, "i am a dog, i am a sub-human animal, i am a dog."

i did all this and waited. i waited for an hour during which time my mind wandered from time to time and i caught myself thinking about a TV program or a book i had read. i pulled him back from this, concentrating on the bars that caged me, on the collar and chain which held me, on the muzzle which took away a lot of my human appearance, on the fact that i was on all fours. i worked at it and sat in the cage panting like a dog.

Another hour or so passed but it was easier than the first. my mind was going down, down and i suddenly realized that i was no longer breathing like a human but panting like the dog i now knew i was. More time passed and more. How long? i didn't know. i yawned, producing a doglike sound almost automatically and naturally, and lay down in my cage. i fell asleep for a while with my head on my paws.

i awoke to find that someone had visited me while i was asleep for there was a large dog bowl filled with water just outside the cage. i got back on all fours and strained forward eagerly to the water, lapping it up and whimpering with pleasure.

The Master entered. He was well built, handsome, powerful, assured. He was wearing a black, military uniform, tall black, highly polished jackboots, and a peaked cap pulled low over his eyes almost hiding the military crop of blond hair. He was every inch a Master, a million miles removed from the dog in the cage in front of him. i began to whine with excitement and tried to wag my rear as if i had a tail. The Master unlocked the cage and as he reached in to release my chains, i the dog covered my Master's hands with dozens of licks and then turned my attention to the boots, almost beside myself with pleasure at the idea of being owned and controlled by this man.

The Master, without saying a word, pulled on my leash and i the dog followed him across the floor, panting and still trying to lick the hands of my trainer. He opened a door and i crawled in behind him into a room all in black with candles burning. There were other men in the room, all dressed in military uniform, all holding leashes at the end of which were dogslaves like me sitting respectfully and attentively at their Masters' feet. i was led to the centre of the circle and my leash was chained to a spike in the ground.

"Gentlemen, tonight we have a new dog to be inducted into this circle. It has had little formal training but already knows the rules that govern a dog's behavior and we shall have to judge for ourselves if it has learned its lessons well and can carry out those rules as a dog should. First, we have to see if it is really in dog mode so we must test it."

i waited in submissive fear to see what would happen to me. First the Master came to me and began stroking me. i feverishly licked the hand that was stroking me and the Master patted me on the head saying, "Good dog." A bowl of water was placed for me a few yards away and my Master moved to it. i sat where i was, never taking my eyes off my Master's face, and although i was thirsty i sat on my haunches , looking up expectantly at my Master, waiting for the word of command. my Master snapped his fingers and i bounded towards him but still i did not drink. Finally, my Master gave me the command and i fell to it greedily. This was repeated with a tin of dog food emptied into the dog bowl and after the command i fell on this too, wolfing it down though i had never eaten dog food before. i thought i might gag at this but in fact disgust is all in the mind - it might be full of unmentionable bits and pieces but it tasted fine.

Suddenly my Master kicked me. i yelped but i did not speak and looked up appealing to my Master - what had i done wrong? The Master kicked me again and i fell down and crawled on my stomach to my Master's boots where i licked them gently, as if afraid to dare this much. my Master commanded me to roll over and i did so, the Master now bringing the sole of the boot onto my dog's snout and i licked it and licked it, wanting to clean it for him, wanting to do anything to show him that all i wanted from life was my Master's favor and praise.

Next i was commanded to sit. One of the other Masters approached with his dogslave and it snapped and growled at me. i whimpered and cowered slightly. i knew that in this assembly i was the lowest, for the others were established dogs and so senior to me. The other dog, still growling, moved round to my arse hole and started sniffing. i tentatively did the same and when the other dog started to lick the hole i did too. It snapped at me again and i cowered at which the dog leapt on my back and drove its cock into my hole. i whimpered a little, still cowering submissively. my Master moved towards me and i crawled over to him, striving to lick my Master's boots again. The other dog fell off me and growled menacingly until it was hauled back by its owner but i did not even notice, so wrapped up was i in the attention i gave to my Master to the exclusion of my own kind, the other dog.

At this point the Master said, "It has passed the tests so far I think you'll agree, gentlemen." They all voiced their assent "It has not uttered a human sound despite provocation; it has eaten and drunk like a dog without any hesitation; and it has submitted to a bigger dog as it in its position should. Finally, it has shown that, whatever interest it might have in other dogs, its primary concern will always be its Master. I propose we now induct it into our society." The others agreed.

my Master placed a chain collar round my neck, locked it with a pad lock and produced three keys which he mangled with pliers and threw away.

"This serves to remind you at all times that you are a dog, you are property, you are owned, and you are controlled."

Leather mittens were fixed on my hands and feet, padlocked, the keys mangled. Pads were fixed around my knees.

"You no longer have the ability to use hands and feet in the way that you used to, even if you wanted to. You wear the pads because you will live on all fours, like a dog. At the end of your week's training you will be branded to mark you irrevocably as property..."

In my cage again i was left for the night, after my Master chucked me a couple of dog biscuits for having passed my first tests. i had more tests to pass the following day....

Part II

i passed an uneasy night. my Master had fastened the chain of my leash to the bars of the cage and had kept it short. The result was i was yanked awake every time that i tried to turn over. Lack of sleep made me irritable. Furthermore, my dog collar was bigger, wider than any slave collar i had worn. Finally i thought, "The hell with it" and worked and worked at unbuckling the collar, no easy task with my hands in leather mitts. Somehow i managed it. i still had the chain round my neck but it gave me no problems. But there wasn't enough space to lie down and i tossed and turned throughout the night, almost disbelieving that i had been so stupid as to get into something as deeply as this. i had no idea when morning came but i was bored and restless by the time my Master appeared.

i had the presence of mind to reach for my leather dog collar as i heard him descend the stairs but i was not fast enough and i realized immediately that, difficult though it had been to remove, replacing it would be impossible no matter how much time i had had. So i was caught with it falling from my mitted hands. He didn't say anything but crossed to the cage and unlocked it. i was suddenly very scared. He towered above me, he was still in his black uniform with the tall gleaming jackboots and from under the brim of his peaked hat i could see fury in his eyes. i hesitated and he said curtly, "Out."

i crawled out, feeling stiff and uncomfortable and when i was out i began to stand up to stretch. His temper snapped. He grabbed hold of me and threw me to the ground, and began kicking me with his boots.

"You useless piece of shit. What kind of a fucking cur are you? Have you learned nothing?"

"Please, please," i moaned, "Don't hurt me." This enraged him even more. "You fucking worthless piece of dogshit. Why the fuck are you speaking? you're a fucking dog and dogs don't speak. Dogs don't stand. Dogs don't remove their collars."

"Hang on a moment please," i cried, "this isn't turning me on any more."

"Turning you on! Do you think that this is what it is all about? It's my turn-ons that are important, not yours." With that he stormed out of the room, locking the door behind him. i lay on the floor, winded and bruised, but not daring to stand up. He was gone less than five minutes, returning with a large canvas bag, which clanked ominously. i edged my way into a corner as if for safety. He moved towards me and towered over me. Diving into the bag, he came up with a different collar, metal this time, snapped it round my neck and quickly locked it. It felt heavy and bulky - there was a small box like contraption fitted on top of it. As he groped in his bag again, i said quietly, "Look - can't we discuss this for a moment?" He glared at me and continued - he fastened a thick chrome collar around my balls. It, too, had a small device fixed to the outside. Pulling me round, he slid a chrome dildo up my ass. Then more conventional metal restraints and chains were fastened to my ankles and wrists and a chain attached to the metal collar. He stood back to admire his handiwork. Now, with an evil grin he brought out a black box from the bag and flicked a switch.

"What were you trying to say, dogslave?" i hesitated, looking at him worriedly. "Go on - what ever it was, say it. SAY IT!"

"Well," i began. i don't think i even got as far as the Ls on the end of the word when terrific pain shot through my neck, my balls, and my ass. i fell to the ground, panting, trying to focus my mind, trying not to pass out with the shock.

"Try again, dogshit." He waited.

"i..." again the pain. i fell to the floor, groaning like an animal for in truth i was incapable of speech.

"Now try barking." i shook my head.

"Bark!" he ordered. "Bark like the fucking dog you are or I'll turn the current up. Bark!" i had no choice - the collar was voice activated; he was digging in his bag to produce what horror i could hardly guess so i barked quietly and fearfully, waiting for the pain to sear through me. It didn't come.

"Louder! Come on, louder, dogturd." i barked louder - still nothing.

"Now whine." i whined - no reaction.

"Pant." i panted - the same.

"Growl." i growled - still nothing.

"Whistle." If i had been thinking properly i would have seen the point he was getting at; but i wasn't thinking, so i whistled. The pain shot through me.

"Any time you make a noise which is not canine, the current will be activated. you got off to a good start yesterday and I thought I wouldn't have to use this device but you have disappointed me and I'm going to have to work harder on you than I thought I would. You've felt the pain and don't like it. Now I'll let you into a little secret to show you how kind I am. I'm not going to ask you to stand up because I'm giving you a chance. If you stand up like a human the pain will shoot through you and will stop only when you are back on all fours like the dog you are. Now get back in your fucking cage, dogslave."

i think i went into a state of shock for a few hours. It wasn't just the pain i had gone through - it was more to do with the realization of what i had let myself in for. When my libido was at its most pronounced (the previous day during the build up to the induction and the induction itself), i was led by my cock and not my brain. i had gone through with something that had always struck me as a hot fantasy; an uncomfortable night had led me to think otherwise but now here i was forced into accepting the reality of it. In my cage i couldn't stand up, of course, so there was no way of testing whether the electrodes did in fact work if i were to try to stand as a human. But i believed my Master when he told me this was the case. i had made a commitment to a life as a dog even though i bitterly regretted it. All of a sudden i realized that i was going to have to work at it with the utmost dedication - and perhaps when my basic training was over i'd be able to turn my attention to finding some way out of the contract. But for the moment i had to concentrate on behaving like a wholly devoted dogslave.

i didn't see my Master for some time - i don't know how long it was as i was kept in my cage in the dark between training sessions. From time to time, someone would come and feed me - always the same coarse dog food out of a tin. And my training began with these unknown men instructing me in the 'basics'. i was taught to sit on command, to 'stay', to 'fetch', to 'rollover', to 'beg', to offer a 'paw'. On the command 'show' i raised my arse, spread my legs, head up, eyes straight ahead, waiting to be inspected. I can't tell you how often these commands were repeated - i seemed to have hours of them every day. Sometimes there would be two or three of these Masters, in different parts of the room, calling out orders as i hastened to obey each of them in turn. Or they would put me in a rest position and then chat amongst themselves before unexpectedly throwing a command at me. And God help me if i didn't respond quickly enough for they all carried training crops and would lay into me at the slightest show of reluctance or defiance on my part.

By way of a 'rest' for me i was given equally long vocal sessions where i was taught to bark in different registers to express different emotions - fear, warning, excitement, pleasure - on and on until i was hoarse. The same went for whining and whimpering, growling, howling. And especially panting - they wanted me to pant, essentially all the time when i was not making other dog sounds. my tongue had to protrude as far as it could, and i had to emulate a 'lolling' movement at all times...

Exercises in body movement were also there from the start. i had thought that, living as a dog, i would have to spend a life of crawling on my hands and knees - and of course i did do a certain amount of that. But for faster movements, my knees had to be raised from the ground, while my 'paws' continued to rest on it, like a runner poised for the starting pistol. But any sort of movement was really arduous, though i was assured that muscles would build in time. i was taught to lie and stretch, flexing my muscles, as a form of relief from the cramped positions i usually found myself in. Tail wagging was another art i had to learn, from diffident, questioning, almost imperceptible movements to frenzied waggling. Funnily enough this became easier on the second day when a dildo with straps with a bushy tail the same color as my head hair (what little they left me) fixed to the end of it was inserted in my arse. This was only ever removed for shitting. i was trained to the leash which was attached to a nasty spiked choke collar - a sharp tug to this ensured my obedience. i was taken outside to a long, cold yard to relieve myself. First i had to sniff for a suitable place, then cock a leg and piss. To shit, i had to curl my back and shit into a hole, always finishing with an appreciative sniff of the ordure. Endless repetition had its obvious result. It began to seem natural. It was as if i had been hypnotized or put into a trance - and yet there was no room for trancelike behavior - i had to be fast, attentive, responsive, constantly alert unless i had been told to 'rest' - even then i had to keep an ear cocked for a sudden resumption of training.

By the time i was placed in my cage at night i was mentally and physically exhausted. But i will say this for these guys - they knew what they were doing. They never treated me as anything other than a dog. They never became in any way emotionally involved - all my training was curt, objective, inflexible, dispassionate. I was praised from time to time but in an offhand, almost absentminded manner. So i learned what they wanted me to learn and yes, my behavior became increasingly instinctive and natural to me. Goaded on by their crops, i struggled to be a total dogslave - for in this i was different from a dog. i had to become truly submissive, more submissive than any dog i had seen, rushing to lick their boots when they appeared, rolling over on my back exposing my genitals, licking the hands that punished me.

How long this basic training went on i have no idea. My only guide was when i was taken outside and this was deliberately confusing - sometimes darkest night, other times blazing daylight - i really didn't know what to expect until i left my training centre. i lost all real concept of time. i imagine it was five days - that's what i think now when i look back because my Master stuck to his word and 'released' me when a week was up. So let's say it was five days. That left two days of specialized training and bonding with my Master alone...

Part III

Chained in my cage, in total darkness, i knew i should sleep as much as possible to be ready for the ordeal that lay ahead but i couldn't help but think back to the first night i had spent in this cage. Then i had been turned on by what i had experienced - until the discomfort of being in a cage for hours at a time had got to me. It was then i had made that terrible blunder of seeking to control my own destiny just after i had formally handed it over to another. Now i had very different emotions to keep me awake.

The cramped conditions of the cage hardly entered my consciousness any more - i was used to that, as i was to the collar around my neck and the various electrical devices that had been used to control, tame and train me. Part of me was apprehensive because i had seen something of my Master's capacity for violence and anger when i disobeyed. But mostly i reviewed the days of training, concentrating on remembering everything i had learned at the hands of the indifferent trainers. i kept revisiting these scenes in my head, playing them over and over. Yet part of me recognized that i was wasting my time. It was no longer a case of me remembering orders, commands, and modes of behavior. These were all 'programmed' in me - i didn't have to think when i heard a command, i simply executed it without the semblance of a thought passing through my head.

But there was one conscious thought sitting at the centre of my mind. i had changed a hell of a lot in the past five days or so but more than anything else i realized that the last of my human behavior - when i took the collar off, when i tried to speak or stand up - these were the last vestiges of my struggle not to accept the submissiveness which lay at the heart of my being. Up to that point i had been playing with the idea of finding the heart of my submission - but it was something that i wanted to put on and off like a coat. i had been brought to the point where i had to confront the fact that i was living a lie in my everyday life - i saw now that my dog life represented my real nature. Before i had come to this place i reckon that 95% of my life was spent in living in the 'real' world and only 5% given over to my slave nature. That had been overturned, i knew it, i felt it in every part of my being. What i didn't know was the new percentages.

Therefore, having been denied even a sight of my Master for days, i was determined to prove to him that not only had i learned all my lessons but that i had really learned my 'big lesson' and wanted nothing more than to be the dog that He desired me to be. Finally, despite all the tossing and turning in my mind, i did sleep long and soundly and contentedly so that i was awake and ready and primed long before he came to me.

And now he was coming. i heard the boots sounding all the way down the hall; then the key in the lock. Quickly i was on my knees, facing the door of my cage, my tongue hanging out, panting and whimpering with excitement, straining at the chain which fastened my collar to the bars. The door opened and He stepped in, locking it behind him. i kept my eyes lowered for, dog though i am; i am also a slave and know my place when confronted with my Master.

He walks towards the cage and now his boots are in my line of vision. At the sight of them, i can't help it - i start barking and barking as if i would never stop.

"Enough!" he says, not harshly but firmly and quietly.

"Welcome your Master, dogslave." He sticks his right boot through the feeding hole of my cage and i fall on it, slobbering and licking and so proud that he has granted me this honor. i lick and lick as if my life depended on it and indeed i have now convinced myself it does. For if i do not measure up to his exacting standards i know i will have failed and the price to pay will be to be rejected, now and forever. Today represents my best chance of finding myself and ensuring my happiness for as long as i live. i will not fail! And so i lick and lick with obsessive concentration, not thinking of the mundane, idiotic things that used to flit through my mind in similar situations in the past - 'How long is this going on for? i wonder if my tongue is getting black....' No, at that moment there is nothing more important than the boot in front of me, now slick and wet. It is taken away from me and i whine in frustration but then the left boot appears and i attack it with even more energy if such a thing were possible.

i have lost all concept of time - i no longer know how much time i spend on any one activity as whatever it is becomes the entire focus of my behavior. Everything seems to pass in a wonderful dream - being released from my cage, showing off my new skills in terms of canine actions and reactions. i have found that space where everything seems easy and natural to me. If i stopped to think i would know just how fulfilled i am but conscious thought has gone - i am instinctively a dog.

Of course, i fuck up from time to time - there is still fine-tuning to be done; i have to learn the subtlety of inflection that my Master uses to convey his exact requirements. And i am punished for these evidences of falling short of the ideal. i am chained by a short length of chain from my collar to a ring on the floor and he whips me; no build up, no special considerations just short, sharp punishment, administered not cruelly but effectively and dispassionately. And i not only bear it without a murmur (or even a whine!) but want it, need it. i want it harder because i know that i have deserved it; i am disappointed that he doesn't whip me harder because there is nothing i would not do or undergo to prove myself worthy of my Master's attention.

He whips me to remind me that i am not only dog but also slave and must be punished accordingly. The tails of the whip lap around my chest or my cock and balls from time to time but, so deep am i in my world of slavery that though they hurt more and would normally provoke me to tears or complaint, they have the effect of making me curl my body into the strokes, relishing their kiss. i say the punishment is short but i suppose what i really mean is that it is all too short for me. Pain is pain - it hurts. When i made my first tentative steps into this type of activity i thought that through some miracle a beating would not hurt. Of course it hurts - especially at a time like now when it is meant to hurt and punish, not titillate. But i want it to send me, i will it to send me, down, down, down into the darkest recesses of my mind where it becomes the purest pleasure.

He knows all this as he whips me because he says (and i can hear a laugh hovering behind his words), "If I ever suspect that you are fucking up in order to be punished; you can be sure I'll devise something much nastier

for you, you pervert scum."
But i know he is pleased with his assistants. They have turned me into the dog i had always toyed with the idea of becoming. His task is to make sure that the slave is not forgotten. And it was to this that he gave his fullest attention after i had been fed chunky food from my dog bowl and spent an hour or so of rest in my cage.

When he returned, he had brought a black leather bag with him. He sat on a chair while i lay at his feet, my chin resting on one of his boots. From time to time his hand would stroke me, or scratch behind my ears. Finally he stood and removed all the electrodes that were still fastened to me. They were unnecessary - i hadn't felt a jolt of electricity in days, it hadn't entered my mind to do anything but behave in a fully dog-like way.

"you have done well, dog, considering how badly you started the training process. you know that you have been brought face to face with your real nature. you know that you are now where you want to be. But the process isn't over yet. Now you must be marked so that all others who use you in the future will know what you are. The chain around your neck will never come off - you already know that. But nor will the other rings I put on you."

So now i knew what was in the bag. my dog training deserted me for a moment as i realized that i was going to be pierced without anything to dull the pain, not even a heightened sense of being a slave which had seen me so well through the punishment beatings. Of course, i didn't react in any overt way but he saw the flash of fear in my eyes.

"you'll endure this for me, slave; without a murmur, without a word as you've been taught. you'll endure it because it's what you want and need. I know you'll suffer through it but you'll be so proud once it's done." He laid his implements out. i could not bring myself to watch because needles have always terrified me. my heart was beating wildly and yet there was a curious sense of calm behind the fear and i reached out to that to help me through. His final act of charity was to gag me firmly - not so much, i imagine, to prevent me crying out or breaking the code that only dog noises should be heard from me but to give me something to bite on, to grit my teeth on.

First my nipples. In a way they hurt the worst because there was my expectation of the unknown to heighten my consciousness. But the sense of a ritual being enacted provided me with a raft of support and as piercing followed piercing i found that i was going down again, that this marking was indeed what i wanted.

Next my cock - a PA; then another just below my ball sac; then finally, a septum piercing and a ring through my nose. By that stage i was back in my world of total abandonment of all control - the place where i most wanted to be. As the ring was inserted into my nose i passed out - not from the pain, i was beyond that - but from what i can only describe as ecstasy. i felt that my journey was at an end and i had finally become what i wanted to be.

But the end never comes when you expect it to. i came to back in my cage - my piercings all freshly bandaged. There was no sign of my Master, no sign of anyone but i could hear a lot of movement beyond the door of the cell that housed my cage. Something was afoot and i knew in my heart that i was going to play a part in it. Had i thought back to my induction ceremony i might have remembered but one of the biggest differences between the old me and the new dogslave was that increasingly i lived in the present, in the here and now. It's the happiest place to be - memory can bring pain, and projection into the future may bring fear of what might happen, of what could happen. This is the secret of a dog's happiness i know now - it lives for the moment and is happy there. And so was i. So the sounds produced no apprehension, just curiosity.

my Master returned. He was in serious mood but calm and purposeful. Without ceremony i was released from my cage and blindfolded. A dog leash was attached to my collar and i was let out of my cell, down a corridor where i sensed other people, other men - i could smell leather. i heard the crackle of a fire. i was led forward and was then commanded to sit. The blindfold was removed and i was back in the centre of a circle of men, some with leashed dogslaves at their booted feet, back in the room where my induction had taken place. Ah yes, it was time for my branding, the final mark that would set me aside from my former life forever.

my Master bent down and carefully, even tenderly, removed the bandages from my piercings. As each piece of tape came off i whined softly for the wounds were so new and so vulnerable. But i remained calm other than this minimal display of suffering. Chains were handed to him.

i almost wept at the sight of these chains. They were lighter than any chains i had yet worn and i knew in an instant that my Master knew he no longer had to impose his will through pain. These were almost symbolic chains - strong enough to hold me, especially when even their slight weight pulled on my piercings, but in a sense unnecessary. i would not have struggled to get away.

For all this consideration they were still real enough. i was being introduced - as gently as possible - to the purpose of the piercings. In the future they would be used to restrain me for punishment beatings. A single chain passed from one to another and were padlocked in place, adding to the pressure on these sensitive spots. All but the ring on my nose which was singled out for special treatment - a very short chain went from it to a ring set in the floor and padlocked there.

i knew what was about to happen and i knew that any movement from me while i was being branded would lead to the piercings being ripped open. No wonder he could forego heavy chains! i was held in place by an instinctive concern for my body, and that i found was more powerful than any chain. But chains have their power too and the combination made a potent mix.

A ritual was being enacted above my head but the words passed through my mind without recognition. my mind was elsewhere. It was revelling in its degradation, in all the marks of its servitude, in its desire for more and more humiliation. So much flashed before my eyes, visions of the cage, boots, the trainers with their crops, my Master's peaked cap, his belt, his whip, chains, dog collar, leash, dog bowl, cocking my leg, my nose ringed, my cock, it too ringed. i felt the heat from the iron as it approached slowly, slowly so that i would be aware of it and not lose myself in anything other than the reality of those few moments. i couldn't see it but from the sheer amount of heat i knew that this was no insignificant mark that would be overlooked in a locker room. HIS mark, perhaps saying, 'dog' or 'dogslave' or perhaps a symbol - i was not to know for another twenty hours or so. And the iron descended on my right arse cheek and as it did my arse rose to embrace it as it burned its mark into me. It seared into me. my heightened senses screamed silently with the sheer intensity of the pain; my soul bucked like a bronco but my body did not betray me and was still.

It was over. my body was aflame with the pain in my piercings but soon they faded into insignificance as the pain of the branding rose above all. my breathing was labored but no other sound had escaped my lips. The chain tethering my nose to the ring was removed. i sank down into my normal dog position and shakily crawled towards my Master's boots. And licked them in gratitude. A cheer broke out and much applause, but i was indifferent to it as my Master raised my head and spat forcefully on my face. i opened my mouth and he spat again, directly into it. Then he patted me on the head, smiled and spat again as my tongue tried to lick as much of the drool as it could.

"you have passed all the tests, you have graduated from the training program, you are marked permanently as the dogslave you are. you now have evidence that you are the sub-human scum you always knew you were, marked forever as my property. Soon it will be time to release you when you have had a day for your wounds to begin healing. you will rest and then I let you go but remember that I can and will recall you at any time to continue to abuse you and humiliate you." Tears filled my eyes. He looked at me and said, "What's the matter? You can speak on this occasion, dogslave."

"Master", i stammered, "please don't send me away. Let me stay and live as your dogslave. Please, Master, please, please, i beg of you..." But what chance had i of changing his mind with human words? As a human i meant nothing to him but as his dogslave... Surely he had not trained me so thoroughly to kick me out now? i sank to his boots, panting and whining, then feverishly licking, willing him to change his mind and keep me with him. There were humiliations he hadn't imposed on me, humiliations i would gladly offer up to him if only he would keep me as his dogslave to use and abuse when the mood took him and otherwise consign me to my cage with its dog blanket and dog bowl and the chains to secure me and give me that sense of being really alive and really fulfilled.

He smiled and said nothing.

But he did send me away as he had said he would.

And i find i lie awake and wait for the phone, above me by the bed where I no longer sleep, cannot sleep. i lie on the floor, collared and leashed, and wait for it to ring and recall me to my proper place.

DOG DREAMS

By holedog

When I was a teenager I dreamed about being a dog, wearing a collar and living in a dog cage.

When I was about 15 years old I had a friend who lived across a large field from me in a farmhouse which had a backyard full of junk, storage sheds, old cars, and animal pens.

His parents had owned several large dogs. In his backyard was a steel pole set into the ground with concrete. Hooked to the pole was a heavy chain about 20' long where they would chain up the dogs at night. Every time I would visit my friend and we would go into his backyard I would be fixated with that chain, fantasizing about me being chained to that pole for the night.

After thinking about it a lot I decided one night to make my fantasy come true. I would sneak across the field, take off all my clothes, get down on all fours and chain myself to that pole. I would spend the night as a chained dog.

It took some time for everything to fall into place, but one summer day my friend told me that his parents were going out of town and that he was spending the night at another friend's house. Now I had it. Nobody would be home and I could spend the night chained up in their backyard totally safe from anyone seeing me.

I told my parents that I would be spending the night at my friend's house (which was the truth) and they had no problem since they were family friends. I went to my room and packed my "overnight" bag. Of course I didn't include any clothes, only a large leather dog collar that I had bought at a feed store and two heavy steel padlocks.

After dinner I left for my friend's house, but because it was still light out I had to wander around for sometime until it got dark. I was still afraid that someone would see me and ruin my fantasy before it started. Finally it began to get quite dark so I crossed the field and squeezed through their barbed wire fence into their backyard. My head was swimming with sexual heat and it had been all I could do to not beat off several times. I kept telling myself that this is what I really wanted and I could beat off once I was a chained up dog.

I walked through the backyard looking for the pole. There it was. Secured in the ground with concrete with no way of removing it. There was the chain all coiled up next to it in some grass. My heart pounded as I began my fantasy. I walked over to a picnic table close by, set down my bag and began to take off all my clothes. It was still quite warm and the breeze felt good against my naked skin. I folded up all my clothes and shoes and placed them in the bag.

I removed the dog collar from the bag and placed it around my neck. It was a heavy, leather dog collar about 1 1/4" wide. It felt tight and stiff on my neck. I took out one of the padlocks and locked the dog collar on my neck. My cock was as hard as a rock by now and I started to beat off. Before I got too far I pulled myself away to finish my fantasy. I removed the second padlock from the bag, double-checked that I had the keys to the padlocks in the bag, then zipped up the bag and set it on the end of the picnic table. I walk over and picked up the chain. It uncoiled and made a loud noise. I looked around but no one was there and the house was dark. Now was the moment I had dreamed about for months. I picked up the chain, took the padlock and locked the chain to my dog collar. I then got down on all fours to begin my night as a dog.

At first my heart was pounding so hard that I thought I would pass out, but after a moment I began to calm down and begin to perceive my new surroundings. I began to slowly feel like a dog. For a long time I just sat there on all fours enjoying the fact that I was chained outside by a dog collar. Soon I began to crawl around the backyard on my hands and knees smelling things. I would go out as far as I could until the chain would pull taught. I would then turn back to explore another direction. There were so many things to investigate that I really got lost in my mind as a dog. I even began to raise my leg and pee on things. Of course from time to time I would stop and begin to beat off wildly, but each time I would stop just before I climaxed and force myself back into my dog fantasy. After a while I curled up and laid down. I looked out across the field at the moon and felt quite content. I could hear other dogs barking in the distance and I felt happy.

By this time it had been about 2 hours and my cock was still rock hard. I couldn't keep my hands off my dick for any longer so I began to beat off. This time I couldn't stop; the feeling of the ground and the dog collar locked around my neck sent me over the edge. I came violently, spewing cum all over the ground and me. Without much thinking I bent down and licked up my cum from the ground. It tasted good, even though I got some grass and dirt in each lick.

As I sat there calming down I began to wonder if I could really spend the night chained up like this. I began to miss my bedroom and it even felt a little cold now. I thought about getting up, unchaining myself and making up some excuse to go home, after all it was still before midnight. Before I could think about it too much though, my sexual urges kicked in again and I decided to remain a chained up dog for the night.

As I looked around I noticed a large dog carrier off to one side. I crawled over to it and it was within the chains reach. I thought "great!" I can spend the night in there. It should be warmer. I opened the metal barred door and crawled in. It was made for a very large dog and was quite roomy. I pulled the door shut and tried to latch it, but the chain connected to my dog collar kept the door from lining up correctly and I couldn't get it to shut. I worked on it for some time and then finally with a little force   I managed to get the latch to go in and the door locked shut.

My dick was throbbing again and I began to beat off inside the dog cage. I came again with an even bigger orgasm than before. Afterwards I again bent down and licked up my cum from the cage floor. This time as I calmed down I decided to try and sleep. It was quite warm and comfortable inside the dog cage so I though I would try and rest until morning. So I laid down and slowly fell asleep dreaming dog dreams all night.

I woke with a start. It was quite bright and at first I didn't comprehend where I was. It all came back when I realized that I was in a dog cage and had a chain attached to the dog collar locked around my neck. Since it was already daylight, I knew I had to get loose before my friend returned home and found me like this. I tried to open the latch on the dog cage but in my haste the night before I had jammed the latch into its hole and couldn't get it to release. I panicked. I struggled frantically for sometime until finally I forced the latch to release and the cage door swung open. I crawled out into the bright sunlight. I soon realized that it was still early and I had time to get out of my predicament and return home, so I casually crawled over on all fours to the duffle bad laying the end of the picnic table.

As I neared the far end of the picnic table all of a sudden the chain pulled taught and I was stopped hard. I was still about 5 feet from my duffle bag at the other end of the picnic table so I figured that the chain must have snagged on something. I turned around and crawled back to the pole. There was the chain, but it didn't seem to be stuck on anything. I figured that it must have tangled up on something, so I carefully pulled the chain out tight as I crawled back to the table. Again at about 5 feet from my bag the chain pulled tight. I sat their on all fours confused. What was wrong? Then it hit me. I had miscalculated the distance from the end of the picnic table to the chain. If I stretched I could just reach one end of the table, but my bag with the keys to the padlocks was laying on the other end of the table. I was trapped!

I stretched my arms and used my legs pulling as hard as I could until I nearly choked myself, but nothing I did gave me enough length to reach the bag. I grabbed the end of the picnic table and tried to pull it towards me, but it was set hard into the ground and I couldn't get enough leverage to budge it. Finally I gave up and sat down almost in tears. The enormity of my situation began to hit me. Soon my friend would come home and see me naked and chained up by a dog collar in his back yard. Worse, his parents were also due home. What could I say? What would they tell my parents? I had wanted to be a chained up dog, but not forever!

I must have sat there for about 20 minutes until all of a sudden I noticed a rake lying in the grass nearby. I grabbed it and pulling as hard as I could on my chain the end of the rake just snagged the bag and I was able to pull it to me. I got out the keys, unlocked the chain and dog collar and put on my clothes. I ran home through the field. I would dream of being a dog another day.

DOGBOY CHEWS STRANGER'S MEAT

by Christopher Pierce

When Mitch first came to stay with us, I knew he would have to have me before he left. And he did.

Mitch was one of my Master's oldest friends. They had known each other in New York when they were both starting their own businesses. When Master got the news that His buddy was coming to L.A. for a visit, He insisted that Mitch stay with us.

I had seen photos of Mitch so I knew he was handsome, but I wasn't prepared for the sight of the hunky stud I saw when Master opened the door.

He was about 5'11" with gray-blond hair and a nice, clean-shaven face. His eyes were bright blue, looking almost silver in the late afternoon sun. The polo shirt he was wearing gripped his torso tight, showing off nicely shaped pecs and a washboard stomach that looked hard as a rock.

Mitch had a big athletic bag over his shoulder so I could see one of his arms flexing nicely. The bulge in his arm was almost as big as the bulge in his pants. From my vantage point, on all fours on the floor, it was right in my line of sight.

I must have stared at his crotch longer than was appropriate because my Master kicked me lightly with His booted foot.

"Get out of the way, boy," He said. "Give Mitch room to walk in here."

Snapping back to my senses, I crawled out of the way and watched the man walk into my Master's apartment. The two men exchanged handshakes and hugs, smiling and laughing like the old buddies they were. Mitch set his bag down and I couldn't help sniffing it. It smelled great, the hot manly smell of gym clothes. He must have been traveling all day.

"This is my dog-slave." Master said. "Say hello to Mitch, boy,"

"Woof!" I said enthusiastically, wagging my naked butt back and forth like a tail. The men laughed as Mitch hunkered down to one knee to be on the same level with me. He put a hand on my head and scratched me like he would a dog. I figured he must know what Master was into, because he didn't seem surprised that I was naked except for a leather collar around my neck.

"How you doin', boy?" he asked.

"Great, sir." I answered. I can speak English if addressed directly, otherwise I know Master prefers dog-speak. "I've been looking forward to you staying with us."

He grinned at me and the sight of his flashing white teeth got my doggy-cock hard. Mitch saw it and reached between my legs, gripping it lightly in his hand. His touch was wonderful, strong and masculine, so like Master and yet different.

"He's a horny one, aint he?" he asked my Master.

"Yep," He answered. "He's always ready to get plowed."

"Is that right, boy?" Mitch asked me. I howled, and they laughed again as he stood back up and walked into the living room with Master.

I got beers for them and they sat down to talk. While I was making them dinner, I noticed Mitch watching me, his eyes roaming up and down my body.

"You always keep him that way?" he asked Master.

"Damn right. Naked and collared is how slave boys should always be."

"Amen." Mitch said.

I heard them clink their beer bottles together in a toast.

"He's one fine-looking boy." the visitor said. My cheeks turned red. Master doesn't usually compliment me because He doesn't want me getting full of myself, so the unexpected praise brought a blush to my skin.

"That he is." Master agreed. I kept my mind on my work, trying not to let their conversation distract me. When dinner was ready, I served it to them at the table before returning to the kitchen for my own meal. As always, I ate it out of my dog bowl with no hands. When I was done I cleared off the table and cleaned the dishes.

After dinner I was allowed to curl up at Master's feet while he and Mitch smoked cigars and talked about old times. It was wonderful to lie there knowing I was the owned property of my Master. Earlier He had scratched me behind the ears and told me how proud He was of me, so I was a very happy boy. I was so content lying at their feet that I fell asleep right there on the floor.

It was pretty late when Master woke me up and said it was time for Him to get to bed. Mitch said he was going to stay up and watch some TV before hitting the sack himself.

Master ordered me to fix up the guest room for Mitch before reporting back to Him in His bedroom. I scurried to obey, getting clean sheets for the guest bed and making the room nice and comfortable for him. Carrying Mitch's bag to the room in my mouth, I even got to smell his delicious man-odor some more.

When the room was ready, I reported as ordered to my Master in His bedroom. He was already nearly asleep. I sat obediently at the side of His bed, sniffing his arm like the curious dog I was.

His hand reached out to scratch behind my ears. Mmmm, I loved it when He did that. It made my puppy-dick hard to have Him touch me with such affection.

"Boy," He said. "Mitch's one of my best friends. He doesn't have a boy of his own right now, and he's really aching to work a hot piece of meat over. I want you to go out there and offer yourself to him. He's a good man, we can trust him." He gestured to a large drawstring sack next to the bed on the floor. "Take that to him. Tell him he can use anything in it." I was looking at the sack, imagining what was making it so plump and full. Master gently took my chin in His hand and brought me back to looking at Him. "And you," He said. "Serve him like you would Me."

"Yes, Sir!" I whispered enthusiastically, wagging my butt.

"Good dog," He said, settling back against His pillows. He'd be asleep in seconds, I knew, so I was careful not to make any noise as I leaned over and picked up the sack in my mouth. It was heavy, almost as heavy as Mitch's athletic bag had been. But I could handle it.

I padded out of the room and on all fours, taking care to quietly nuzzle Master's bedroom door shut on the way out. The apartment was dark. The only light was the ghostly reflections on the walls from the TV in the main room.

Squaring my shoulders, I crawled down the hallway toward the light, toward Mitch. As the TV came in to view, I could see that it was no late night talk show our houseguest was watching. Two gorgeous stud-pups were filling the screen, humping each other and stroking each other's cocks. Mitch had discovered Master's collection of porn tapes.

Coming around the edge of the couch where he was sitting, I saw that Mitch was far from sleepy. His eyes were wide open, and he had pulled his dick out of his pants and was jerking it off. It was a beautiful cock, not really long, but wide and firm, the foreskin gone to reveal the powerful head to the world. Shining with lubrication, his erect penis looked like a glowing talisman in the dark.

Mitch glanced over at me with a surprised look on his face.

"Hey, boy," he said. "You scared me for a second. C'mere." I dropped the sack and crawled over him, rubbing my head against his leg affectionately. "Thought everyone was asleep. What did you bring?" he gestured with one hand at the sack while he petted me with the other.

"Master told me to offer myself to you, Sir." Out of the corner of my eye I could see his cock flex at the words. He got a big smile on his handsome face.

"Is that right?" he said.

"Yes, Sir." I reached over and pulled the sack close, picking it up in my mouth and holding it out for him. He took it, holding it on his lap. "He said to tell you that you can use anything in that sack on me, and that I'm yours for the night. I'm to serve you as I do Him."

Mitch leaned back, the smile on his face getting bigger and bigger. I could tell my news pleased him greatly.

"Well now," he said. "This is what I call hospitality. Let's see what we've got here."

He opened the sack to look inside and the grin on his face got bigger and bigger. I could read his expression as clear as day: Relief at last!

Then he put the sack aside and leaned back, pushing his body further down on the couch. His cock jutted up, looking magical in the strange light of the TV. It made me salivate just seeing it.

"You can start by serving my dick, puppy-boy." Mitch said.

"Oh, thank you, Sir," I whispered as I maneuvered myself between his legs, my mouth enveloping his gorgeous cock-head. I forced myself to savor it, to stay there, enjoying just the feel of that bulb of hot man-meat. Stroking it with my tongue, it seemed as if it came alive in my mouth, growing and pulsing with pleasure and excitement.

"Mmmmm..." Mitch murmured, putting his hands behind his head in a gesture of utter satisfaction and contentment.

Little drops of pre-cum started to ooze out of his piss-slit, and I lovingly slurped them up. He tasted so fucking good -- again, like Master but also very different. My doggy-dick was standing straight out, hard as a rock at the incredible intensity of serving this hot man.

I couldn't hold back anymore and started to slide my mouth down over his shaft, letting the head move back further and further until it hit the back of my throat. Still hungry, I tried to get even more of him inside me. I managed to almost reach down to his pubic hair. His dick was so intense, like a throbbing hot iron in my mouth, except that it didn't burn me with fire, it burned me with passion.

Mitch put his hand in my hair and, grabbing a gentle fistful of it, guided my head into a wonderful up-and-down motion, not too fast, not too slow, but just how he wanted it. I obeyed his non-verbal command, imitating the action and speed so precisely he let go of me and put his hands behind his head again.

I sucked his cock slowly and deliberately, cherishing each stroke down towards his crotch, every stroke back up towards the head. I felt full and complete, because I was getting used by this totally hot stud, being used like the dog-slave I was, used to bring pleasure. I wondered what could possibly be more fulfilling than this...

As my sucking continued, Mitch sat up and pulled off his polo shirt, letting it fall to the couch. Although my angle was not the best, what I did see of his torso made my knees weak. My earlier guess had been right...that tight shirt had been concealing a physique of utter perfection, sculpted and molded as if carved from stone.

He reached into the sack and pulled something out. I couldn't tell what it was in the darkness until he leaned forward over my shoulder. His strong, powerful hands found their way to my crotch and took hold of my balls. They felt utterly trapped in his grip. I felt completely in his power, like he could crush my balls in a heartbeat...like I would do anything for him. And I would. I had my orders.

But even if I hadn't, serving this man was second nature to me. I was a born slave, and knew that worshipping men such as Mitch and my Master was why I had been born.

Then both of his hands were in my crotch, pulling something tight and around my extended balls. He had pulled my ball-sack out from my body, and was now wrapping whatever it was around the newly exposed base. I realized what it was, then, and reveled in the feeling of the leather thong binding me. Tightly he knotted the thong, keeping my balls stretched far out from my body. My cock bulged in ecstasy, its tip already slick with pre-cum.

Mitch left himself a long trailing loose end of the thong, which he used as a leash when he sat back. Now he had me by the balls, and could pull and stretch them at his whim. As if I wasn't already completely in his control, now I was bound, captured by him. One yank of that thong, and I would drown in a sea of pain. As always, the fact that another man had that power over me, that I was helpless, was intoxicating to me.

"Oh yeah..." he moaned as I sucked his dick harder, the pain in my crotch as he pulled on the thong making me more and more incensed.

Suddenly he was sliding forward, dropping off the couch onto his knees in front of me. His cock slid out of my mouth, a long trailing tentacle of saliva connected us until it snapped apart. Now Mitch's chest was right in front of my face, and his powerful muscled arms were going around me, squeezing me tight.

"Good boy," he whispered. "Good dog...you make me feel so good."

I wagged my butt in happiness, and I heard him chuckle. Then he dropped the thong and, taking my head in his hands, kissed me hard and fast and firm on the mouth. Instantly his tongue was inside, probing and searching and dominating me from the inside out.

Wanting to be totally open to him, I willed my throat to open even further, to show him that my whole body, my whole soul, was his to explore and use however he saw fit. His kiss was passionate, wonderful -- forceful and yet tender, both rough and sensual.

Then his mouth was moving, leaving my lips and traveling, sucking and biting as it did. He trailed down my neck and onto my chest, settling on my left nipple. Little yelps of pain/pleasure came out of me as he worked my tits, alternating quickly between biting and caressing. His tongue swirled around the sensitive skin, then he was chewing me, gnawing on

59

the nubs of flesh like they were tasty treats. He squeezed me again, tight.

"Good dog," he whispered in my ear. "Good boy..."
I whimpered in response. Human speech was no longer adequate to express how I felt. The smells of him: sweat, musk, day-old deodorant and cologne...were spellbinding, electrifying my mind just as much as his touch did my body.

Then he was moving upward. I closed my eyes and put my face forward, connecting to his body with my mouth. My lips and tongue left a trail of saliva on him as he stood up to his full height. Our houseguest wiggled out of his pants and let them and his boxers fall to the carpet.

Looking up to him, his magnificent cock stood straight out from his body. It cast a huge shadow on the wall. But the stud-pups on the TV had outlived their usefulness for Mitch. He picked up the remote and clicked off the TV and VCR.

"Time to hit the sack, boy." he said.

He reached down towards me and with one hand gripped me around the wrist. Pulling me up to my feet, he slung me over his shoulder like I was just a sack of laundry. He used one arm to anchor me in place while he reached down with the other hand to pick up Master's sack. Tossing the sack over his other shoulder, Mitch headed for the guest room.

Even with my cock and balls tied off and painfully smashed against the man's shoulder, it was totally hot. I love getting carried by guys - it's so primitive and possessive. My puppy-cock was raging by now.

Mitch carried me into the guest room and shut the door behind us. Then he set me down on the bed that I had so nicely made a few minutes before.

"I've had my eye on you since I first showed up," he said, reaching into the sack and pulling out a leather penis-shaped gag. "Don't want to wake up your Master," he said as he slowly stuck it inside my mouth. I stared up into his beautiful eyes as he did it. It was so intense, he pushed the gag into my mouth with the same sensuality and animal heat I could imagine him pushing his cock into my ass.

Hopefully I wouldn't have to wait long for that.

He tightened the straps around my head and fastened it tight. Now even I did make noise, it wouldn't be loud enough for anyone to hear. Next Mitch pulled a pair of handcuffs out of the Master's sack. Expertly he locked my wrists together in front of me.

Mitch pushed my hands over my head so my armpits were open to the ceiling. Now I was vulnerable and helpless.

"Just keep those hands out of my way, boy." he said.

I moaned obediently into the gag and the muffled sound brought a smile to my user's face. What he did next surprised the hell out of me. Somehow that made it even hotter than if I had known it was coming.

The hot stud man leaned over and took my hard puppy-cock in his mouth and started sucking me like a pro! Now I was trained the old-fashioned way, that only slaves and bottoms sucked dick. That tops acted and bottoms got acted on, so in all the time Master had owned me, I had never gotten a blow job.

But there was one rule I learned that was more important than any of the others, and that rule is the reason I didn't freak out completely when Mitch, a consummate top, starting slurping on my tool. I was a slave, and slaves are made to serve, and serve however their Master sees fit. I had been ordered to give myself to this man, and if this was how he wanted to use me, that was his option.

It felt unbelievably good, besides.

Man, his mouth was wonderful, smooth and hot like electric satin on my desperate dick. The suck-job didn't last long. It was more of a tease than anything else. But for the seconds Mitch blew me I was in pig-heaven.

Mitch pulled off my cock and put his hands on me. He explored my abs and chest, probing and searching, like a blind man whose only way to experience me was tactilely. His hands moved over every inch of me, passing over my erect nipples and making them shiver.

"Mmmm..." he muttered as if savoring fine wine. "I haven't had a slave to work over in a long time..." It was almost like he was talking to himself. I was overjoyed to be there for him, to be available for whatever he wanted to do to me.

Then he climbed on top of me and laid down. He wasn't as heavy as my Master, but feeling all that solid muscle on me was wonderful. I felt trapped, held down, confined...things that make a lot of people disturbed and frightened, but that I totally got off on.

Mitch started moving, grinding his big top-cock against my pecker. His mouth was on my face, kissing my eyelids, his tongue flicking in and out like a reptiles', every touch of it like a brush with fire. The man gripped one of my wrists in each of his hands, pinning them to the bed. As if I was going anywhere! But this added restriction got me ever more horny and hungry for him to use me.

Humping me harder now, every stroke burned against me as our steel-hard cocks got mashed together. His panting breath was in my ear. I could hear him getting more and more excited.

Suddenly he was grabbing me by the waist and flipping me over onto my stomach. Immediately I stuck my ass up in the air. I wanted him to see how much I wanted to serve him, how open I was to his every whim. If I hadn't been gagged I would have been whining and crying like a bitch in heat, dying for him to screw the shit out of me.

But the houseguest had other ideas, as I could see when he reached into the sack again, this time coming up with a rolled flogger. He unfurled it, the leather thongs hanging down like twenty rat-tails.

Mitch planted his dick between my butt-cheeks, resting it on top of my ass. This, of course, was maddening, and I pushed myself up and back, as if I could somehow get him inside me on my own. He chuckled quietly and played with the flogger, dragging the tails across my back and down the trail between my shoulder blades. Every stroke drove me deeper and deeper into sexual hysteria, silently crying out please whip me! please fuck me! please use me!

The cock on my ass was heating up, moving slowly back and forth without entering me. I whined and moaned into the gag. Then the flogger began to hit me, lightly at first, then harder and harder. smack! Smack! Smack!

Mitch hit me with the flogger and tortured my ass with anticipation. I could feel his body moving rhythmically, but if the stud was moving to music, it was a song for his ears only.

The blows on my butt and back were hurting now, like little bursts of fire, flashing brightly and fading quickly, to be replaced by more seconds later.

"You know what, slaveboy?" Mitch asked suddenly.

I made a questioning noise through the gag.

"I don't think you're ready for this yet." he said and pulled his pulsing cock away from my ass. Shaking my head violently, I made desperate pleasing noises I hoped were communicating no please no I am ready I AM ready! It was absolute torture to feel him pull away from me. He stopped flogging me, and I collapsed on the bed, breathing heavily.

Still on my stomach, I couldn't see what Mitch was doing behind me, but I did hear him rummaging around in the sack I'd brought him. A moment later I heard the squirt of a lube bottle being squeezed.

Something new was between my butt-cheeks now, and I realized it was a dildo.

A big one.

"Yeah, this is better," the stud growled. "You weren't quite ready for my stud-man's cock, were you?"

"Yes, Sir!" I tried to say through the gag. "I'm ready for your stud-man's cock!"

But Mitch had made his mind up, and nothing was going to change it. He worked the dildo up and down my ass-crack, teasing me, as if I wasn't already excited enough! What would it take to please my horny houseguest?

I moved my ass around, moaning and crying, trying desperately to communicate, to let him know I was ready, that I needed to be taken, that I needed to be penetrated!

Please Sir I'll do anything just please take me!

Mitch yanked at the thong that held my balls in its tight grip and pain seared through me. I must have been making too much noise, because the stud on top of me said "Shut up, dogboy. Quit whining and crying like a she-bitch or I'll leave you right where you are, and you can just think about what you've done while I get some sleep. You can just sit there, all open and empty, waiting for a cock that won't come. And you'll have plenty to answer for when I tell your Master how I disappointed I am with you. Then you'll be shit out of luck, won't you?"

I nodded slowly.

"Now you gonna behave? Gonna be my nice hungry quiet dogboy?" he asked as he yanked the thong again. I swallowed the yelp of pain and nodded again.

"Good." Mitch said. "Now we can get back to the good stuff." He released my balls and picked up the dildo again. I heard him slather more lube on it and felt him resume using it on my butt.

This time the strokes were more direct, less teasing. I flexed my ass muscles, trying to open myself as much as possible, to provide best possible assess for my welcome intruder. When Mitch was ready for injection, I was as prepared as any boy could be.

The dildo's sculpted head nosed its way inside me, easily popping past my sphincter ring and into my most private of places. My houseguest pushed, and the simulated penis moved further into me. He pushed more, and soon enough I had the entire dildo inside me, with just its base sticking out.

Mitch's low heavy breathing was wonderful to hear. It sounded like he was getting off on this as much as I was. My own forgotten cock rubbed against me, trapped between the bed and my groin. He fucked me with the dildo then, pulling it out then pushing it back in - my ass made delicious slurping noises as it gripped the plastic penis.

"Turn over, boy." he said above me. "But keep the dildo inside you." He pushed it until its entire length was in me, to make his order a little easier to carry out.

Holding my breath, I clamped my muscles around the invading dildo. Then I began to turn myself over, from resting on my stomach to resting on my back. Mitch maintained his grip on the tool he was fucking me with, and it was sweet bliss feeling it stay in place while my body rotated around it. When I had turned completely over, my hard dick was exposed, dripping pearly drops of fluid onto my abdomen.

"That's what I like to see." Mitch said as he yanked my dick away from my body and let it smack painfully back. "Now I can see your face, I can see your eyes." This seemed particularly important to him but I didn't know why.

He ran a hand down my arms, my muscles straining in the cuffs that held them above. His hand found my nipples, tweaking each one in turn. All the while he was still fucking me with the dildo. This went on for what seemed like a long time, every torturous second piling up.

It was wonderful to be used and stimulated like that, but I hoped it was only prelude to the real fucking that was coming.

Finally Mitch seemed to tire of the game. He put the dildo aside, and went into the sack one more time. I recognized the packet he fished out - the shiny square of a condom package was unmistakable.

Mitch removed the wrapper and unrolled the condom down the shaft of his nice big pecker. The whole time, his eyes never left mine, he seemed to avoid breaking out eye contact at any cost.

No time like the present. The big man grabbed my legs and tossed them up over his shoulders. With a clear shot at my quivering hole, he shoved himself forward. The muscles of my rectum greeted his cock with relish, tightening up not to keep it out, but to keep it inside me.

He fucked me. Deep, hard and strong. Beads of sweat formed on his forehead and dripped down onto my face. I hungrily licked up the ones I could reach with my tongue.

It was heaven to be used this way, by Master's friend, just to be there for him to make use of however he wanted. I was just another piece of Master's property that he could loan out to a friend, like a valuable book or a car...

Before I knew it, I felt Mitch's body tense up and I knew he was shooting off inside me, the condom catching all his spunk and holding it prisoner, just as Mitch was holding me prisoner.

I was his, I realized. Mitch's.

Even if only for a short time, I belonged to this man, even if only for a second, a heartbeat was all he needed to completely and utterly own me in every possible way.

And in that instant, his eyes boring into mine, he grabbed my cock in his fist and jerked me

once.....twice.....three times

and I came. Intense ecstasy flowed through me as jizz flooded out of my rod, landing thick and milky on my pectoral muscles. The man whose dick was inside me sighed long and hard, caught his breath and gently pulled out. Moments later, with the condom and its contents flushed safely down the toilet, Mitch climbed back in bed with me.

"That was just...perfect." he said. "Just fucking perfect." He reached between my legs and carefully untied the cord that encircled my balls. Relief coursed through me, and it was intense prickly pain as blood flowed back into my balls.

Mitch took the gag out of my mouth with a grin. "You won't be making any more noise tonight, boy." he whispered, and I nodded in submission. He left the cuffs on my hands, pulling himself into the circle of my arms. Now we were bound together literally. It was absolute heaven having this

hunky stud snuggle in close to me, but I was fading fast. As I drifted away I heard him whisper "Go to sleep, my boy, go to sleep..."
I slept the slumber of contentment, satisfied that I had performed as ordered.

Mitch left the next day, after giving a full report to my owner. Master beamed with pride as he hugged his friend and wished him well.

"You're welcome to stay here any time!" He said.

"I'll be back!" Mitch said as he threw his bag over his shoulder. "You can count on it!"

After he was gone, Master scratched me behind the ears.

"Come on, boy!" He said. "Time for your reward!"

GAY PUPPY

by White Collar

Foreward:

    I read the story "Puppy" by Jrad and, though it was not gay, the combination of human K9 and Mind Control was irresistible. I wrote the author and asked him if he'd either consider writing a gay version or, alternatively, if I could set it as a gay story. He said he wouldn't mind if I did it, since being straight, he had no inclination to write a gay story himself. So I've recast the story in a gay rendition, adding a few "gay" things, but mostly just changing the sex of the hypnotist. I hope you enjoy it and many thanks to Jrad for the premise and his kind permission to make use of it.

GAY PUPPY

I opened my eyes, and immediately knew something was wrong. It's hard to describe, but I was very clear, and at the same time confused. For starters, I couldn't talk anymore. I wasn't gagged, or mute, I just didn't know any words or how to use them. I opened my mouth in a parody of what I knew was speech, and made sounds as I moved my mouth, but it wasn't words. I knew it wasn't real words.

Somehow I was aware that I could still understand perfectly well what people said; I just couldn't talk any more. Puppies can't talk. Puppies have to wear collars, and crawl on the floor, and grovel and live their lives as someone else pleases. I knew that I was a puppy now. Not a normal kind of puppy that had been born one, but somehow I'd been made into one.

My body didn't look like other puppies bodies, but that didn't change anything. How did I know this? Why was it so obvious to me what I now was? I didn't know. My puppy body was completely naked; I knew it shouldn't be. I was cold. All the hair on my body was gone, even around my puppy peter. I used to have hair on my chest, but it was gone too. I didn't know when, or why it had happened. All I knew was that even though I used to be a person, a man, I wasn't any more. I used to do lots of things; I'd mated with women. I'd been in business, but now I couldn't walk or talk like a person. I had to crawl and whine, and bark. It's all I knew how to do. That time before was like a dream.

I tried to stand up, but couldn't get very far before I'd lost my balance and got dizzy. No, puppies stay on the floor. Puppies crawl. Oh God, what was happening to me? No, what had already happened to me? How does a person just open their eyes, and know they aren't human? How does that happen? I still looked like a person, but looks didn't change the truth. An involuntary whine of fear escaped me at that moment as if to punctuate my non-humanness.

No, this isn't real, I thought desperately. I don't want to be a puppy! Please no, I was meant to be a person. I don't want to be this. Of course I didn't say any of that, just thought it. Not even in words really, but just mental pictures, and feelings. I sobbed out loud, and was startled to feel tears rolling down my cheeks. I reached up to wipe them away, and realized that I couldn't open my paw anymore. No, not paw it's my... Oh no, what is it called? I have to remember. Not paw though! It's definitely not a paw. Anyway, I couldn't open it up anymore. It used to open up, and I could do things with it. Pick things up, and make my front toes wiggle and curl around things. Front toes? That doesn't sound right either. I'm probably just being paranoid. What else would they be called?

My thoughts were interrupted as the door opened and he stepped through. I knew him very well, but who was he? I knew who he was now, but who was he before? Now he was the one who was in charge of me. The one who controls me, and makes me do what he wants, and takes care of me. Puppies can't take care of themselves. My heart sank. No, puppies can't take care of themselves at all. But who was he before? I don't think he had always been in charge of me, just like I don't think I had always been a puppy. But I could no more remember him before he was my Master than I could remember myself before I was a puppy.

I was so ashamed to have him looking at me. Seeing that I wasn't a person anymore. Seeing him watch me, and know what I was. I wanted to die. I wished he would stop looking at me, and now what? He's smiling at me. Oh why is he doing this to me? Why is he doing this to me? I weighed this question, and suddenly realized that it meant much more than I thought. I realized that it was he who had made me be a puppy; he who had taken away my right and ability to be a person.

It enraged me, and humiliated me even more that this was his doing. But what could I do? How does one change what they are? I looked at him, and he was smiling an amused smile at me. I crumbled, and lowered my face unable to look at him anymore; the weight of my shame pushing me to the ground.

He slapped his knees with his hands. "Here boy, come here puppy, come on boy!" He said to me in a jolly but condescending voice, and I hated him for talking to me like that. But how else would he talk to me? He wanted me to come to him, and that's how you talk to puppies isn't it? My face felt hot, and my ears burned with humiliation as I tried desperately to fight the urge to go to him. Something about the way he coaxed me, and the sound of him slapping him knees just made me naturally want to go to him despite my torment. I was strong though. I didn't want to give him the satisfaction of controlling me, and I stayed put. I fixed my paws on the ground, and didn't move.

He saw that I wasn't coming to him; that I was fighting it with all my will, and an even more amused smile spread across his face. As he started to dig in his pocket, I began to think, he was in charge of me, but also took care of me. What if I made him mad? How would I eat? When would I get to go potty? Not potty, what's the real word for it? Oh damn! Why can't I think of any of these important words? What if I made him angry, and he decided not to feed me? What would I do? Would I starve to death? My resolve was about to break. I was just about to crawl to him when he produced what he had been digging for in his pocket.

I looked at it in horror for a moment. It was a hard rubber chew toy; a red bone, and I was afraid, no panicked to realize that I wanted it. I couldn't look away from it as he moved it back and forth like a hypnotist with a pocket watch. My eyes were glued to it. I couldn't look away. I had to have it. Oh God PLEASE let me have it. I forced my gaze to break away from it so I could look up at him face with my big puppy dog eyes; my begging, sad puppy dog eyes.

I crawled very quickly to him, and sat in my most obedient attentive puppy posture. My legs layed out behind me, my haunches resting on ankles and my paws placed firmly on the floor in front of me. My puppy peter and balls rested on the cold concrete. I looked up at him, and whined pitifully. I wanted the bone so much I couldn't stand it.

"Oh you want this?" he said in a very mocking tone of voice. I sat up on my haunches, and let my front paws dangle before my chest. I whimpered louder several times, and considered snatching it out of his hand with my teeth. He was holding it very close to my face. "I shouldn't let you have it because you have been a bad boy not coming to me when I called. Don't you know puppies have to come to their Masters when they are called?" he asked. I barked and whined at him desperately, my eyes glued to the chew toy.

He moved the toy behind his back, and my heart stopped. Oh no! "Now I want you to be a very good puppy for Master. I want you to do everything Master says, or I will take this away, and you will never see it again. Do you want that to happen?" he asked. I whined as if I had just lost something dear, and laid my head on the ground. He smiled very broadly. "I didn't think so."

The next thing I knew, the bone was on the floor in front of my face, and I snatched it in my teeth. I bit down on it, and was in heaven and hell. I hated this. I didn't want to be doing it, but I had to chew it. I had to gnaw, and bite, and play with it. It was an absolute compulsion, but it made me sick with shame.

He watched me very amused, and chuckled. "What's the matter puppy? Can't stop chewing it even though you want to? Well puppies are ruled by their compulsions don't you know?" I began to cry as I gnawed at the toy. I had never been addicted to any drug before, but I imagined this was what it was like. To have equal amounts of hate and need at the same time.

He knelt down beside me and started to pet my head. This too was humiliating, but at the same time it was pure ecstasy. The hair stood on the back of my neck, and my whole body tingled. I shivered with pleasure, and the last tear ran down my cheek as I drifted away on a cloud of delight. I could stay like this forever. I didn't care that I was a dog, this was warm safe comfortable place and I loved it.

Suddenly I was shocked back into reality as the bone pulled out of my teeth. It was a moment before I realized that he had taken it from me and was putting it in a drawer near by. I was horrified. No! He couldn't do this! I'd die! I whimpered, and then began to growl. This got him attention, and he snapped around. "NO! Bad boy!" he scolded. His voice was so loud, so commanding it almost hurt my brain to hear it.

He took a rope and tied it around my neck and pulled me to a large chair and tied the rope to it. "You're a bad boy!" he said again and went back out the door he'd come in, leaving me all alone. I sat there on my haunches, looking at the door. Where was he? Had he left me? What was going to happen to me? I needed him; I really wanted him. He talked to me; he smiled at me. He made me feel wanted. I started to whimper, sad that I'd growled at my Master. I couldn't imagine going against his voice. Whatever it ordered I must do. I'm sorry Master. Please come back! Please! I began to call to him to come back and my voice rose in a long, drawn-out, pitiful howl.

After a long time, the door opened and he came back in the room. I was overjoyed and yipped with excitement, rearing up on my haunches and pawing the air with my front paws. I wiggled my rear end with joy I was so happy to see him again. When he saw my reaction to him, he softened and was all sweetness and smiles again. "You're going to be such a good puppy. I'm so glad I have you now," he said, patting me on the head as I licked his leg and hand. He saw my rump wiggling back and forth and gave me a playful swat. "I can see that I need to get puppy a tail. Every puppy should have a tail!" he said. I tried again desperately to think of who he was. I knew him very well, but he hadn't always been this. I hadn't always been this to him. How long ago had he changed into this all-powerful being? Or was it that I'd changed into a powerless creature? I didn't know and thinking about it made my headache.

"Let me give you something else to chew on. Maybe you were weaned too early and need something to satisfy your need, poor puppy." And he patted my head condescendingly. Then he pulled down the front of his pants and pulled out his peter. But it wasn't at all like my little puppy peter; it was big and hairy and stiff. "Come here boy!" he said and I had to go to him because I wanted it so bad and I wanted to please him so bad. I don't know why; I don't understand it. I'd never had a man's peter in my mouth before, but I needed to have it. He held it in his hand and patted his leg. "C'mon. Up boy!" I sat up on my haunches, my front paws dangling against my chest and opened my mouth. I looked at it hungrily and my mouth watered. "Good boy," he cooed and put his peter in my mouth. "Now you can suck on it. That's a good puppy." I sucked and sucked, trying to relieve my need. I licked its shiny red knob and licked at the slit where a wonderful salty fluid came out. As I did, my puppy peter began to get harder and longer and bumped up against my trim belly. "This will be a nice snack for my puppy," he said. "Suck on it now!" and I took it in my mouth and sucked hard. After some time, I was beginning to get tired and started to whine. "It won't be long puppy. Just a little more." Soon, his peter throbbed in my mouth and my puppy mouth was filled with a bitter salty liquid that I swallowed quickly. I wanted it and didn't want him to take it away from me like he had my chew toy. So I swallowed it and licked his peter clean to get every drop.

"Good boy!" he said. "Now sit! I still need to name you, and I can't decide yet." My face turned red at this. Need to name me? I have a name. I've always had a name it's...It's...Well, he knows it. Why is he saying he has to name me? You can't name someone who's already named. Can you?

"Rover is my favorite so far, but it's just such a classic dog name that lots of the other masters are sure to name their puppies Rover too." I almost threw up at the realization that if he named me that I'd have to answer to it. I'd have to constantly acknowledge that my name was in fact Rover. This can't be. He can't call me that please!

"Of course, there's Fido and Rex too, but they have the same problem. I don't want ten doggies perking up and coming to me every time we're the park and I call your name now do I?" My stomach churned at the thought. He was going to name me something awful. Some stupid demeaning name that degraded me constantly, and I couldn't do anything about it. And what was that about the park? He was going to take me to the park? He'd take me outside like this? Where people could see me?

"But don't worry, Master has already come up with the answer." He produced a brown leather collar with big black letters on it. I could see them clearly, but couldn't read it. For a moment I wondered if it was another language or something, but the characters were far too familiar for that. The plain fact was I couldn't read any more.

"Oh I'm sorry, I forgot doggies can't read." He said as he buckled it in place around my neck. "It says 'Bobo'. Your name is Bobo." I died a small death inside at hearing this. "I know it sounds kind of funny, like a clown, but I think it's cute too. You look like a Bobo to me, and so you are."

The strangest thing was that every time he said the word Bobo, my attention sprang to him. My eyes fixed on him and for a few moments I couldn't look away. I could hardly hear anything else, and briefly it seemed like the rest of the world had blurred some and become dim. Whenever he said my name, it was like he had a leash connected to my mind and he'd just yanked it hard. I was incapable of ignoring it, and every time I looked at him, I knew it was as if I were saying. "Yes, my name is Bobo, and I am a dog." Every time he said my name "Bobo", I forgot a little bit more of "before". "Before" was fading away. I wanted to die. I felt like I was dying, but I knew that my new life was just beginning.

Goodpup

by goodpup

goodpup writes:

Thank You very much Sir for publishing my story, A real buzz to see it up there. i hope it brings pleasure to a few guys, i know it has to me, and my Master is intent on recreating every detail in one night now Sir, ouch!

i also have a piece of a memoir from when i first arrived in New York in 1985 i think You might be interested in. It is an accurate description of how i met my first real Master, although of course the dialog etc are all recreated, and i can't recall exactly what we did, though the meeting in the bar and the run up the stairs are forever (happily) etched in my memory.

Goodpup

I had arrived there in November, after a month of pretty wild sex in San Francisco. 24, hot and horny, ready to party and there I was in New York. AIDS was there too of course, but people weren't talking about it much. I don't recall seeing condoms anywhere. More a dread rumor that terrified us so much that we couldn't bear to look it squarely in the face.

So there I was. The Mineshaft was open, The Anvil and the St Marks Baths too, as well as the constant street cruising, Sex just seemed to be everywhere I looked, and I liked that. But I wanted more than just sex.

I had already had a fair bit of BDSM training when I was 19 and living in Australia for a year. No full time Master, but a few older guys who took an interest in me, if you know what I mean. On return to New Zealand, it had been hard to break into that world - I guess there weren't many guys into it then, or I looked too young or something. Still, I managed to get a bit of non-vanilla action here and there, but I knew what I really wanted. I wanted a Master, an Owner, and I couldn't find that in Auckland.

San Francisco had been better that way. I'd met a few guys, had a few good, hot scenes, but I didn't want to stay there. New York though, somehow it spoke to my heart as soon as I saw it.

The Mineshaft was incredible. I think one guy on the door had a little crush on me; he always used to tease me and joke when I got there. I was too shy and young to know how to respond though. But that's not where I met my Master.

It was a bar somewhere in the Village. Can't recall the name now. It had a little cramped bar in the front with a few tables, and a tunnel like backroom running down one side of it. I went there a fair bit. I was sitting in there one cold night, leather pants, white T (I'd taken off my sweaters) and leather jacket, Doc Martins. I guess I looked pretty tasty sitting there like that, but I still felt like a shy gangly boy from a long way away. Must have looked a bit unsure too, trying to look tough and experienced in New York.

This guy walked in. Taller than me, about 6'2. He was truly one of the most handsome men I have ever seen. Tall, built, broad-shouldered, elegant and commanding. He had on a trench-coat and a well-cut suit underneath. He didn't need any leather or chains - he just radiated sex and power. He had that presence about him. What they call a Roman head, with close wavy hair. He ordered a drink and looked around, then came and sat down at my table. He didn't ask if it was alright, just sat down and said "hi".

I couldn't believe it. I couldn't think of what to say to this god sitting next to me, but stumbled out a greeting in reply. He picked up on my accent right away, and asked where I was from. England? No I told him and had to explain where New Zealand was. He seemed amused. Why was I sitting in this particular bar he asked me. I told him how I liked sex, and sex of a certain kind, and certain kinds of men, and he smiled. I remember I went for a cigarette, and he leaned over and took one himself, then lit them both from his Zippo. Again, no explanation, he just did it. He looked at me and grinned. "So what ya into boy?" he asked. I blushed, and stuttered something incoherent. He gripped my chin and looked me in the eyes "Ever played hard before boy?" .I nodded. This was unfucking believable, but it was happening to me. He leaned over real close and whispered into my ear, "I'm one mean motherfucker, and I am not joking, got it?" then leaned back, a big smile on his face, looking like he'd just told me a great joke. He kept on grinning, and then held his big, bronzed hand out to me across the table. "Kiss it" he instructed me, and I did, without even stopping to think. "Good boy, now follow me" he said, and I did.

Out we went and he hailed a cab. We headed to somewhere up on the West Side. A part that seemed to me like it was just beginning to go up in the world again, but I can't recall exactly where. "You are going to do everything I tell you too" he said to me in the cab. "You don't stop to think, you just obey. You'll find out just how far you can trust me later". I was electrified with that incredible mix of terror and excitement, shaking in my boots.

"When we get there, I'm going to pay for the cab. You're going to run up the stairs to my apartment on the fourth floor, and I'm going to give you a minute. By the time I get there, you are going to be stripped naked and kneeling on my doormat, got it?" I nodded, too scared to say anything else. With one hand he was casually squeezing one of my tits, hard, as the cab moved through the traffic. He took my cigarettes and lit one, and kept the packet, not giving me one. It felt the most natural and perfect thing to do.

We got there, and I tore off up those stairs as fast as I could go, realized when I got there that there were three other doors opening onto the same floor, but what could I do? It was pretty late by then, after 1 in the morning, so I was pretty safe, but didn't feel it. I had been told which one was his, and started to strip as fast as i could. I cursed my 16 hole Docs, they took so long to get off. My leathers which had seemed so sexy and tight now seemed a positive danger. If I wasn't naked by the time he got there... My terror increased as I heard him coming up the stairs. Somehow I made it, just. Naked and trembling, I was there kneeling on his doormat, my clothes in a heap beside me.

He ignored me as he fumbled for his keys. He opened the door, stepped inside and shut it! I was left outside a strange apartment, naked and scared! I was a weird mix of anger, terror and sorrow. "The fucking prick! How could he! I'd kill him, " I was thinking, when the door opened again and he had a collar and dog-lead in his hands. Later I learned that he kept it behind the door, so it could only have been shut for a few seconds, but the effect was incredible. Even more amazing was the fact that I was still there, where he had left me, with no instructions. He reached down and fastened the collar around my neck. "Get in here boy, don't want you scaring my neighbors"

He pulled me in, then gathered up my clothes and boots and dumped them on the floor. "Stand up" he commanded. I stood and looked at him. He spat right in my face and said "Don't you ever look me in the eyes again unless I give you permission. You look at my chin or my feet, or anywhere I tell you, but you are nothing, you have no right to look me in the face. Do you understand?" I mumbled yes. This was not ok. "What?" he said, quietly but so very threateningly. "What did you say? If you speak to me, you speak clearly and firmly and address me as 'Sir' - got that boy!" "Yes Sir!" I answered this time, my eyes fixed on his chin.

He went over to my pants and went through the pockets, tipping the loose change and crap that builds up in them, then opened my wallet, tipped everything out, bills, credit cards, everything. "Shit" I thought to myself, "He's going to rob me." but he just swept it all onto the floor with the clothes, so much more rubbish he seemed to be saying.

"OK, follow me boy." We went into his bedroom, a typically small New York room, big enough for a double bed and a small table, built in wardrobe, not much else. The bed had a low wooden frame around it. He made me stand beside the bed, then fitted a leather parachute around my balls, leather cuffs to my ankles and wrists, then told me to lie down on the bed, face down. I did. He fixed my wrists and ankle cuffs to hooks at the corners of the bed. I was stretched out, not too bad, but it wasn't comfortable. Then he grabbed the chain at the bottom of the parachute and fixed it to a bungee cord that hooked into the middle of the bottom of the bed frame. Fuck that hurt, I couldn't move, couldn't breathe without feeling my balls being pulled tight. He shoved a pillow under me to push my arse up. "I like to see what I'm working on" he said. Then I heard him moving around, then suddenly he shoved a dirty piss-smelling jock-strap into my mouth. I was gagged, bound, with my balls being stretched out behind me feeling like they were on fire. Helpless. I felt him stroke my arse, softly. "Nice butt boy. I like working a butt over. It's kinda white now. I think I'll change the color of it a little first"

There was some more noise behind me, like he was rummaging in a bag or something. Then suddenly, pain! A loud smack! He chuckled as I bucked." Now I think you should try and lie still or you might rip your balls off, but hey, I don't care about your balls so you do what ever you want" Then he went back to work, paddling my arse. That first blow had been pretty hard, but the next ones were much softer, then slowly building up to a stronger and stronger beat. By this time I was freaking a bit. I mean, I had been pretty stoned when I met him, and here I was in a strange apartment, hardly knowing anyone in NY, with a guy whose name I didn't know, totally helpless, and he DID seem like a mean fucker. I was used to some rough stuff, but it was suddenly sinking in to me just how vulnerable I had made myself, and I didn't like it. All the while he was feeding me poppers, which I loved, but also added to my confusion. He stopped paddling my arse, and laughed "Whew, pretty pink arse now boy, you won't forget that in a hurry" then he got up and went to the door, turned the light off and pulled the door nearly shut.

I lay there, not knowing what to do or expect, not able to do anything really, scared. I heard him talking on the phone to some people, the TV went on. Some kitchen noises. The TV went off. No word from him. Then the front door opened and shut. He'd left me there. Now I really began to freak, to panic. But I couldn't do anything, helpless. This also marks the start of my urge to be tied up and left, helpless, at my Master's mercy. He was back in about ten minutes I guess; of course it felt much longer. I never felt so happy as I did when that door opened. He came straight in to me and sat down on the bed, stroked my arse and started talking to me in a low even voice" Scared huh? Yeah, well maybe you should be, little boy like you going home with the first stranger that he meets, you're asking for trouble." All the while he was stroking my arse, hot and sore from the paddling he'd given it. Then I felt him lube my arsehole up. I was still spread out on the bed, my balls still being pulled behind me, smelly jock still in mouth. I was whimpering, almost crying, but I wouldn't let myself cry, refused to. I was scared, but he was being nice to me now, sort of. Now of course, I realize how his tactics worked. Scare the shit out of the slave then be a little bit nice to him, this makes him extra compliant and grateful, and terrified of upsetting the Master. It's an effective tactic.

I heard his pants unzip and come off, then the rest of his clothes, carefully put away in the wardrobe, not dropped on the floor. Then he was on top of me. He was big, and strong, and he had a big fat cock too. He put his arms under me and found my tits, then started working them over, forcing me to buck, being pulled in all directions, by the manacles, the parachute, the pain in my tits, my painful, hot lubed arse. I could feel his dick between my buttocks, feel him pushing it, searching for my hole, then he found it, and he was in! In and fucking me, deep and hard. Man could he fuck! He loved fucking, and went at it for what felt like ages. All I could do was lie there and take it. But I loved it, through all the pain and terror, I was now able to really understand what one of my trainers in Melbourne had told me one night about changing your pain into the master's pleasure, and how that is the way for the slave to really enjoy these scenes, through giving up his will to the Master's pleasure. Now it made sense. Now I really understood what other guys meant when they had told me of going into that slave mind; that sub-space. It was incredible, a turning point.

Eventually, after some very long deep fucking, and with a loud shout, he came, shot all the way up me. I swear I could feel his cum hit me inside, and it was great. We lay there a bit, then he released me, rolled me over, looked down at me and spat in my face again, with a smile. "Good boy" he said, "Good fuck, nice arse. Shower time now" He pulled me up and held me as I found my balance. That felt good, his big body holding me like that. Then he took off the restraints and pushed me through to the shower. He pushed me in first, told me to kneel, then let go with a long hot stream of piss all over me, especially in my face and my crotch. It was great. Then he got in. I really got to see how good his body was then. Hard, cut. A big fat cut cock. I helped him wash, soaping him up . He told me he was 28 and (typical New York) an aspiring actor who did modeling and also worked as an escort, sex for money. I remember he looked at me and said "But you I am doing for my own selfish pleasure, no cash, Hope you appreciate how lucky you are boy". We cuddled and kissed a bit in the shower, which was nice.

I helped rinse and dry him off. We went out, and he told me to get dressed. I'd sorta been hoping to stay the night, but knew I couldn't push it. I told him a little more about myself, feeling elated by what had just happened, and scared it was never going to happen again. When I was dressed, he told me to kneel in front of him. I did. He dropped a small pad and a pen at his feet and told me to write my number down. I did. Then he told me to lick his boots, slowly and carefully, including the soles. And I did. After a while, he told me to stop. He walked over to the door and told me to crawl across the floor to it. I did. Before he opened it, he told me he would call me in a while, and I had better be ready. He also told me I was never to come through this door on my feet, only on my knees. Then he opened it, and told me to go. I left. But I was happy, he said he would call me, he had told me to only come through his door on my knees. I was walking on air. This was one of the best nights of my life...and I knew I would be back for more.

THE GREAT CHASE

by mongrel

The house stood as a monument to everything that was dark and brooding. Like a towering Temple of Decay it stood silhouetted against the clouded night sky. Its early Victorian architecture lent it an eerily Gothic appearance. Tall spindly spires, mounted on top of rounded tiled roofs, pointed like accusing fingers at the sky. From where it nested in an upper story window an old Barn Owl hooted and surveyed all before him with judgmental seriousness. A cold wind swept over the house and a shutter banged against a wall.

The windows, those of which were not shuttered or barred were molded and covered in a thick layer of dust and grime. Thick heavy cobwebs hung from the cornices and drainpipes, and tufts of brown dead grass poked up from between the porch floorboards.

In days long gone by, this house would have been a place of warmth and life. Perhaps housing a family. Freshly painted rooms and halls would have echoed to the sound of children's laughter, and the smell of fresh baked bread would have permeated the walls. But now, it stood silent and alone. Seeming to sigh sadly as the wind howled through it's guttering.

Inside, the rooms were deserted and empty. Odd abandoned pieces of furniture lay scattered about or stood like brooding ghosts covered in white drop clothes. In one room on the second floor a large painting lay propped up against a wall in the corner. A bundle of dirty rags had been stuffed under the painting and a figure lay curled on the rags.

A searing flash of lightning cut the night sky and the figure hunched down and buried his nose in his elbow. Quietly he shivered and watched the first smatterings of rain make speckled patterns in the dust on the windowpane outside.

The rain fell. It poured, bucketed, and did everything else rain does.

Kaleb pulled the car to the side of the road and peered through the foggy window. He looked at his map then back at the crooked old street sign that stood like a skeletal arm in the stark white glow of the headlights.

"Well" He sighed."2045 Rantberry Terrace, this is the place." Kaleb was almost afraid to look.

He had seen the "FOR SALE" advertisement in the Trading Post and had arranged with the owners to view the property. They were out of the country so he agreed to walk through the house by himself. Now as he turned and looked up the winding driveway with it's rough-hewn stone archway and wrought iron gate he wondered what he had let himself in for.

"In for a penny, in for a pound I guess," he said, looking at the big rusted key in his hand. From the way that the gate hung crookedly on the stone pillar he guessed that there was no way in hell he was getting the car through. So pulling up his collar he grabbed the flashlight out of the glove compartment and opened the door. The rain hit him like icy needles and the wind whipped around him sending his coat flapping. Quickly he crossed the road and slid in through the gap in the fence.

It wasn't possible to see the house from the road due to the tangle of trees and vines that grew in the grounds. But Kaleb had a feeling that he was in for one heck of a shock. Keeping his head down he trudged up the driveway. The trees seemed to reach out in the light of his flashlight, grabbing for him. Long tendriled fingers dragging across his face.

The driveway wound slowly up hill until it eventually emerged into a small overgrown courtyard. A crumbling fountain complete with peeing cherub stood in the center of a circular carriageway. Garden beds with similar statues lined the walkway. And just beyond, perched on the hilltop like a brooding black monk, stood...THE HOUSE!

Slowly, with an almost tangible sense of foreboding Kaleb crossed the carriageway and stepped up to the front steps.

Unbeknownst to Kaleb, a dark silhouette watched his progress from where it crouched in the trees at the edge of the driveway.

Another bolt of stark white lightning illuminated deep brooding features, and a heavyset brow furrowed into a permanent scowl. A long jagged scar ran from nose to chin across the right cheek, and the corner of the mouth twitched into an evil sneer. Kaleb most certainly was not alone...

From a room in the steeple tower at the top of the house, wise eyes looked down. Wise knowing eyes. They also noted that Kaleb wasn't alone.

Kaleb wiped the dust from the rusted door handle, and taking the key from his pocket he wriggled it into the keyhole. He applied pressure but the key refused to budge. Bracing himself he pushed harder. Slowly with a dull grinding clunk the key turned in the lock. The old wooden door popped back slightly indicating that the long disused lock had been freed. The wind howled around Kaleb as he took a breath and grasped the rusted door handle. Half a slow turn and the door began to swing slowly open. It creaked loudly as it did so reminding Kaleb of an old horror movie. The torch beam cut a column of strong yellow light into the house beyond, falling on huge cobwebs and sending sparkles of glimmering light along the strands turning them into miniature indoor fireworks displays. Kaleb was instantly hit by the heavy odor of dust and mold. It lay thick everywhere. Coating everything. He stepped into the Foyer and looked about.

The room in which he stood was almost semi circular in shape. Doorways lead off to the left and right and a huge black wood staircase inlaid with what would have once been rich vermilion carpet wound in a graceful arc up to the second floor balcony. Tall stained glass windows followed the stairs up to the second floor, giving it a decidedly Gothic Cathedral appearance.

Above him hung a massive crystal chandelier. Once it might have reflected all the colors of the rainbow down onto the room below it, but now its ornately etched crystal teardrops hung dull and soiled in the darkness. At intervals around the walls, paintings hung. Some in bad disrepair, while others surprisingly showed little or no sign of age at all.

A gigantic round carpet of beautiful embroidery stretched across the floor under Kaleb's feet, and a mirror easily 12 feet high, surrounded by a framework of delicately scrolled cedar stood to the left of the main door. Kaleb could hear his heart pounding in his chest. Slowly he crept across the rug to the stairs. Then one at a time he moved as quietly as he could upwards. He was not sure why he tried to be so quiet. But the silence was like a magical spell that he was sure any alien noise would break. From somewhere above him, a cold wind blew, rustling a tapestry that hung from the wall at the top of the stairs.

A sudden flash of lightning sent blinding shafts of white light cutting through the darkness. Kaleb blinked as the interior of the house was momentarily thrown into stark relief. The beam of his torch shook from the trembling of his hand and he realized that his knees were very close to knocking.

At the top of the stairs he paused to decide where to go next. The second floor balcony stretched out on either side of him. Six identical doorways ran down the wall in front of him. These must be the bedrooms and studies.

"So much for quaint little doer upper," he grumbled under his breath as he stepped up to the first door. It was already slightly ajar so he simply reached out and pushed. It creaked slightly, and then swung quietly open. He was about to step in, when there was a bump, and the sound of something hitting the floor from the end of the hallway. Kaleb spun about and shone the torch in the same direction.

"Hello?" He called in a small voice. When there was no reply, he mentally smacked himself in the back of the head.

"Get a grip stupid," he chided himself. "There is nothing in this big old house that's going to hurt you."

With that he turned back to the room he was about to enter and stepped in through the doorway. The room beyond was exactly what he had been expecting. A bedroom. Complete with a cloth covered bed and furniture. Kaleb relaxed slightly.

"This isn't so bad," he thought. "In fact it's quite cozy. I know a million people who would give their eye teeth for a place like this." He moved about the room surveying this and inspecting that. Running his hands over walls. Checking floors. As bad as it looked it was still pretty good structurally. He would come back tomorrow when the rain had stopped and have a better look. But for now he needed to get back to town and his nice dry hotel room. Moving back out the way he had come, he made his way back to the front door. It was still pouring outside so he pulled his collar high around his neck and stepped out.

At a careful jog he crossed the courtyard and made his way back down the driveway to the fence.

The sight that greeted him could definitely have been better. There stood his car, just where he had left it. The only difference now being that a lumbering spruce tree had uprooted and come crashing down on the hood. The front windshield was smashed and the entire hood was caved in. In addition to this, the right front wheel was completely flat and badly buckled.

"JESUS CHRIST" he yelled throwing down the torch. "MY CAR." He ran around the scene of destruction taking in the damage. To all intents and purposes, the car was a write off. It was going nowhere.

"GOD DAMN!!" Kaleb cursed, " What the hell am I going to do now?" He stood staring at the car, gathering his thoughts for a long time in the rain before he finally decided.

"OK this isn't a total write off. I have insurance. I'll just grab my phone and call for tow truck."

"WHAT DO YOU MEAN TOMORROW MORNING IS THE EARLIEST??" Kaleb screamed into his phone.

"Sorry mister," the tired voice spoke back, "Can't do it before lunchtime tomorrow."

Flames erupted from Kaleb's ears and horns sprung from his forehead. "BUT I AM STUCK IN THE MIDDLE OF NOWHERE!!"

"Sorry mister," The voice apologized none to sympathetically.

"FINE TOMORROW IT IS THEN!" He clicked off the phone and slammed it onto the front seat of the car.

He stood staring into the darkness...Seething for what seemed an eternity before, without a word, he flung open the trunk and grabbed out the picnic basket and bedroll he had brought with him and stalked angrily back up the driveway with torch in hand. This was going to be a long night.

Back in the house, Kaleb returned to the room that he had viewed earlier. It was on the second floor, so it was up out of the damp. And it was pretty much central on the balcony. He unrolled his sleeping bag on one of the beds and set about arranging himself for the night. Half an hour later he sat warming himself by the flickering fire that crackled in the fireplace.

The rain beat a steady rhythm on the roof outside. But the fire held back the cold. Kaleb sat wrapped in his sleeping bag, his clothes drying on the back of a large old chair by the fire. Sitting back he started to take better stock of the room he was in. It was pretty much empty save for the bed, the chair, and a chest of drawers. The one thing that did catch his eye however was a large portrait that hung dusty and forgotten over the fireplace. It was the image of a man in his early thirties or there abouts .He was tall. Verging on thin. But his features were strong and angular. And his eyes held a defiant kind of fire. Even in the painting it was clear to see that he had been a strong willed man. Kaleb stood and moved closer. He reached out a hand and brushed the dust away from the bronze plaque at the bottom of the frame.

"Preston Wainwright," he read out loud.

The instant the words left his lips, the lower window in the room banged open and the wind and rain howled in. Kaleb ran over and pulled the window shut. Then locking it, he returned to the fire.

The temperature in the room however continued to spiral down. In a matter of moments, Kaleb's breath was fogging in front of him, sending billowing clouds of mist up into the freezing air.

Then something entered the room. No doors opened, and nothing was visible, But Kaleb could feel it moving slowly towards him. He stood before the fire trembling as the force circled slowly about him. When it passed the fire, the flames seemed to whither and die. Only to spring back into life as the effects moved on. Kaleb was cold and hot at the same time. His hands shook, and sweat beaded on his forehead. The presence seemed to stop before him. Then, for just the merest fraction of a second Kaleb imagined he saw the smoky outline of a face. Then it was gone.

The room returned to normal temperature and it was as though it had never happened. A moment later...Kaleb breathed

---

He was still standing stunned in the middle of the room when he heard the noise. It was coming from downstairs.

FOOTSTEPS!!

Slow heavy footsteps. Dragging their way across the foyer. Then a bang. Then nothing. Kaleb rummaged through his possessions and found his torch. Then pulling the sleeping bag closer around him, he crept out onto the balcony. As quietly as he could, he moved up and looked over the railing. There below him was the foyer, just as he had left it. Empty and silent.

"Hello," Kaleb called in a small voice, "Who's there?"

When his only reply was the howling of the wind outside, he started slowly down the steps. The torch beam cutting through swirling eddies of dust as he went. In the foyer he stood listening intently. There was a soft clang from the back of the house. Perhaps in the kitchen. He turned and shone the torch down the dark hallway.

"Hello?" He called again. He was answered only by the quiet creak of a door.

Shining the torch on the door Kaleb saw that it was slightly ajar. It had been opened very recently.

"I HAVE A VERY BIG DOG!" Kaleb called out.

He edged his way along the hallway to the door.

"AND HE LIKES TO BITE!"

Again a soft clanking noise from the other side of the door. Kaleb licked his dry lips and took a breath. With a slight push the door swung open. The torch beam cut through the darkness illuminating the room beyond in an eerie yellow glow. The sight that greeted Kaleb made his heart pound with fear and his blood turn to ice in his veins.

Splattered over the walls in big scrawling letters, painted in a thick red substance, were the words. "GET OUT NOW."

Suddenly every horror movie that Kaleb had ever seen came crashing in on him. Chunks rose in his throat and his stomach churned as he watched the letters drip slowly down the tiled kitchen wall. Gripped by fear to big to reason with, Kaleb fled back along the hallway and up the stairs to his room. Slamming the door he locked it and leant gasping against it. His mind was in a vortex of fear. This kind of thing only happened in movies. Suddenly there were footsteps outside his door. The same heavy dragging footsteps he had heard earlier. Kaleb's heart stopped in his chest. He listened; sweat dripping from his brow.

Then BANG!! The door shuddered violently with a fierce blow. Kaleb reeled back, too scared to scream. His eyes glued to the door he huddled in the far corner of the room. Slowly, as he listened, the footsteps moved off down the balcony. Agonizing moments later Kaleb staggered shaking to the door and listened.

NOTHING.

Quickly he pulled on his pants and shirt and grabbed his torch. He had to get out. He didn't know where he was running. All he knew was that running was better than sitting still. Taking a breath he opened the door a fraction of an inch and peered out. The coast was clear. Quickly he walked out onto the balcony and down the steps. He was almost at the bottom when something rustled the tapestry at the top of the stairs behind him. Yowling like a stuck bush pig, Kaleb sprinted down the last of the steps and across the foyer to the front door. Almost insane with fear he flung it open and rocketed out into the darkness. The ice-cold rain hit him square in the face. Blinding him. He half ran half staggered down the porch steps and he was about to cross the courtyard when a dazzling flash of lightning split the darkness. Kaleb saw standing before the fountain, haloed in a ghostly white aura from the lightning, a towering Black figure. It stood between him and the driveway. At almost the same instant a dreadful, chilling howl cut the night air echoing off the walls of the house. Kaleb screamed and turning ran back into the house. He sprinted up the stairs to his room and after locking the door, curled himself into a tiny ball in the corner. Wrapped once more in his sleeping bag he lay trembling with fear and cold. The torch clutched like a weapon to his chest.

Morning arrived and Kaleb slept on. Sometime in the night he had finally given into his fatigue and slipped into a troubled dreaming sleep full of demons, ghosts, and headless ice-cream vendors. The torch slipped from his fingers and hit the floor with a dull clunk. Kaleb sat bolt upright. Ready to run, scream, cry, or a combination of all three if needed.

Warm morning light flooded in through the window and birds sang happily in the trees outside. Kaleb stretched and looked around blinking. He was still huddled in the corner. But now, the terrors of the night before seemed somehow distant and surreal. He stood and rubbed his neck. He was stiff all over but aside from that none the worse for wear. Then he remembered the Writing on the kitchen wall.

A moment later, he hit the hallway on the first floor of the house at a run and burst in through the door. There was the wall. White tiles, but no bloody threats. Nothing but the empty white tiles. Suddenly he felt foolish. He smiled to himself and mentally kicked himself in the butt for having been so childish. Chuckling he made his way back out to the foyer and out onto the porch. Rain still dripped from the gutter, caught like sparkling flashes of crystal in the sunlight. He was still smiling to himself when he saw a man walking up the drive.

He was tall and dressed in a yellow rain jacket and hunting boots, a large shotgun nestled under his right arm, and a pipe stuck from his down turned mouth, leaving a thin trail of blue smoke behind him. He stopped at the foot of the steps and looked at Kaleb.

"Good morning," Kaleb smiled.

"MORNIN'," the man grunted back.

Kaleb saw a long jagged scar running down the man's cheek.

"My name is Kaleb Johns," Kaleb said holding out his hand. "I came last night to look at the house, but my car was hit by a falling tree and I had to stay."

"Jacob Morrison," the man said grasping Kaleb's hand. "I live in the hut at the foot of the hill."

Jacob's eyes never left Kaleb's. And his face remained in a half twisted sneer. "You interested in the house then?" He asked almost accusingly.

"Yes" Kaleb answered. "Well at least I might be. After last night maybe not."

Kaleb laughed but Jacob continued to look serious. "Why is that then?"

For the first time Kaleb noticed the thick Cockney English accent.

"Oh nothing really," Kaleb replied. Waving a hand to dismiss his last comment. "I just heard some noises and got a little spooked is all."

Jacob's brow furrowed even more. "This is a dark place Mr. Johns. Dark and some say dangerous." His eyes flickered from left to right as though he were making sure they were alone. "Some say this house is cursed."

Kaleb raised an eyebrow disbelievingly. "Cursed?"

Jacob leaned in closer and Kaleb smelt the overpowering reek of tobacco. "There are those what say the last owner died in mysterious circumstances," he lowered his voice to a whisper, "he hung himself one night. No one knows why...but ever since then, people have claimed to have seen him walking the grounds on dark nights, and still others say that they hear him moaning and walking through the house."

Kaleb laughed nervously. "OH Really?" He said. "Well I guess there is room for the two of us...It's a big house after all."

Jacob squinted one eye at Kaleb. "Yes...well...that it is Mr. Johns. Lots of rooms to get lost in. I'm not saying I believe it...but it never hurt anyone to be careful."

Kaleb felt a slight chill go down his back. And his breath caught in his throat. He wasn't sure whether it was from the story, or the man's breath but in any case it didn't matter. In a few hours his car would be fixed and he would be gone.

Jacob stepped back. "Anyways...I have business." He tipped his finger in a salute and turned to go. "Good day to you Mr. Johns."

Kaleb watched him go.

"Curiouser and curiouser" He thought to himself.

Then shaking his head he went back inside.

Kaleb looked at his watch. He had nearly 4 hours to wait before the tow truck was due to arrive. And then of course there was the all too real possibility that it would be late. So he definitely had some time to kill. He quickly decided that a further inspection of the house was needed; so starting at the front he worked his way through the ground floor rooms. He had been through the lobby and one of the downstairs parlors when he next came to what appeared to be a small library. For the most part the rotten shelves were empty, but in the lower section of one set of shelves stood two worn volumes.

Large and leather covered they appeared more neglected than old, and on close inspection Kaleb found the oldest of the volumes to be a mere 6 years old. They both appeared to be journals of some kind, although the ink had faded for the most part, and the gently rolling handwriting was almost impossible to read.

One entry however caught his eye. It read as follows.

"14th September 1994. Today I signed the last of the estate over to my beloved. He will now be the rightful protector of all that is his. My illness continues to worsen, the doctors say I have only months to live. I worry more than I should what will happen to him once I am gone.

He will fend for the house...but who will fend for him. I have hoped that a suitable successor would appear before I died. But it seems that such is not to be the case. In the event that I die before my task is complete. I will entrust the will to him to hide and throw his fate to the winds of hope and chance...I pray they are listening."

A sudden chill swept over Kaleb and he closed the book. He felt suddenly as though he were intruding. Looking down upon a small part of a much bigger picture. Carefully he opened the other book and found it to be empty save for a receipt on yellowed and brittle paper made out to Jacob Morrison for services rendered.

As well he found a list of transactions under the same name. Monthly payments right up until the 24th of September 1994.

Kaleb made a mental note that he would have to ask Jacob about them when they next met. Closing the book, Kaleb stood and stretched. His left leg had fallen asleep. And as he was massaging the life back into it, there came from his room upstairs a loud THUMP!

Quickly Kaleb grabbed up the first thing he could find, which happened to be a very heavy iron candle stick that stood in the corner of the library and made his way quickly back through the lobby and up the main staircase to the second floor balcony. The door to his room was ajar, and from within he could hear the rustling of paper. Slowly he crept forwards making as little noise a possible. Holding his breath, he reached out, and grasping the door handle he braced himself. Then, in one quick motion, he flung wide the door and charged into the room wailing and waving the candlestick wildly above his head.

The room was empty. But his possessions now lay strewn about the floor. All his food had been rifled through and his clothes were spread in every direction. Someone, or something, had most certainly been in his room.

---

12 Noon came and went. And there was still no sign of the tow truck. Kaleb made his way back down to his car to retrieve his phone. Only to find that in his anger he had smashed it beyond all hopes of operation when he had hurled it onto the front seat of the car. In addition, the rain had soaked it. It was now little more than a slightly ugly...but very expensive paperweight.

It was nearing 6pm when Kaleb, finally sick of waiting, pulled on his jacket, and started out in the direction that he was hoping Jacob's hut laid. The yard sloped gently away from the house and soon descended into thick pine forest. The heady scent of pine needles mixed with wet earth and pollen. Kaleb followed a tiny winding dirt path down through the trees. The last molten rays of sun cut beams through the tree branches, making dappled patterns of light dance across the wet forest floor.

Kaleb came to a small bubbling stream across which was built a tiny wooden bridge. It seemed to Kaleb like a picture from an old fairytale he had read when he was very young. Away, and further down the hill he could just make out the top of a tiny thatched roof. As he drew closer he saw that it was a small ramshackle looking cottage, once whitewashed walls now faded and yellowed with age perched almost oddly amongst the towering pines and spruce trees. To one side of the cottage stood a small stable now disused and forgotten and on the other side stood a pile of freshly cut fire wood, neatly stacked in rows up to Kaleb's shoulder.

"HELLO" Kaleb called stepping up to the front door. "ANYONE AT HOME?" The door creaked open at a push and Kaleb peered in. "MR MORRISON" He called. He stepped in and looked around.

The tiny one roomed abode was cluttered and dusty. Save for the flickering lamp on the table against the far wall. And the disheveled bed in the corner there was no indication that anyone had lived here for a very long time. All about the floor were strewn odds and ends of tools and instruments of every shape and kind. A pile of old newspapers stood in one corner on top of which perched an old wicker birdcage. In the birdcage, broken and useless lay an old camera. Why anyone would want to cage a camera was beyond Kaleb...but he had learned better than to ask.

On the mantle above the small fireplace there stood an array of odds and ends. A cracked mirror, a worn leather boot, and a small ragged looking teddy bear. This caught Kaleb's eye and he picked it down and turned it over in his hands. It was not very big and was missing an eye. But for some reason it seemed not to fit with the rest of the rooms' objects. Somehow Kaleb just couldn't imagine a man like Jacob Morrison owning a teddy bear.

There was a sudden metallic clank from outside and Kaleb quickly replaced the bear over the fireplace. "MR MORRISON," he called stepping outside. It was nearly completely dark now. And the air had taken on a sudden chill. Kaleb could see no one anywhere around the hut.

"MR MORRISON" he called again. "I wanted to use your phone if I might but, it appears you don't have one."

There was another rustle from around the corner of the house and Kaleb froze. There came...following the rustle a deep-throated growl. Kaleb's eyes bugged out of his head. Trembling he raised his fingers and made a cross.

"STAY BACK" he warned. His voice trembled and broke with his rising fear. He saw something move in the underbrush. Something big and dark. "I have a gun you know?" Kaleb croaked. "And I don't mind using it either." He had already begun to back away.

Suddenly the ground sloped behind him, took a steep step down and he stepped out into thin air. Not looking where he had been backing to, Kaleb's foot waved for a moment before, with a cry. He toppled backwards and rolled end over end down the slippery wet slope. He stopped eventually and scrambled to his feet, spitting out leaves and sticks. He was now in waist high underbrush. Thick green ferns created an almost complete cover, shielding the forest floor from him. Suddenly away up the hill the ferns began to tremble. Shivering in a wake as something charged towards him down the hill.

Kaleb drew in a breath to scream then as suddenly as it had started; when it was no more than a meter away...it stopped. Kaleb suddenly knew how a swimmer must feel when he knows a man-eating shark is stalking him. He peered nervously around him. Straining his eyes into the dense underbrush for any sign of movement. There was none. Then, without warning there was a rustle directly in front of him and something heavy and solid brushed against his leg.

Yelping, Kaleb leapt to one side. He saw the Fern wake move away from him then turn in a U turn and head back towards him. Not waiting to think twice...Kaleb turned and at a full sprint fled away through the trees. His heart bounded in his ears, but he could still hear the thumping footsteps and the crashing of the ferns right behind him as he ran. "OH GOD" he prayed, "OH GOD OH GOD OH GOD!"

He ran until his breathing was little more than ragged gasps, then suddenly something caught his ankle and he stumbled. He yelled as he fell and something heavy hit him squarely on the back. They rolled. Kaleb and Demon attacker together. Kaleb opened his eyes and saw fern leaves and earth flashing passed him. He yelled as he rolled somehow hoping that it might help. Somewhere in their descent the two got separated and Kaleb slammed side ways into a thick spruce trunk.

He lay winded for a moment before he staggered to his feet and once more began to stumble on through the forest. He had no idea in which direction he was going. He just knew that he needed to run. Ahead of him a tree branch seemed to whip out and slapped him across the face. He cried out and veered away up the hill. Muddied and scratched he crested the top of the hill and burst out into the courtyard of the house. Trembling and whimpering he staggered across the carriageway and up the porch steps into the house. He slammed the door shut behind him and raced up the stairs to his room.

Out in the yard a soft low chuckle wafted quietly across the breeze, content in its own little joke, and completely unnoticed by all involved.

Kaleb sat huddled on his bed. This place was an insane asylum...he thought to himself. That was the only possible explanation. It was now painfully obvious that the tow truck people had forgot him...and with his phone broken he had little or no choice but to wait out the night once again and hike back down the road in the morning. Taking deep gulping breaths he tried to calm himself.

"Find something to eat," he thought. "Take your mind of this crazy house."

He clambered off the bed and rummaged through his backpack...all he had left was a packet of wiener's and a slice of bread. Well, wiener's and toast it was then. But first he would have to light the fire. And that meant scouting for wood. So arming himself with a heavy iron poker from the side of the fireplace he set out in search of something to burn.

Downstairs, the basement window creaked open. First one booted foot came through. Then another. They scrabbled about for a moment before they found a purchase on an old crate. Slowly Jacob lowered the rest of himself through the window and onto the basement floor. Then, being careful not to make a noise he dragged in a large pile of rusted chain after him.

Chuckling quietly to himself he set about his fiendish work.

Kaleb found an old chair that was rotten and broken in one of the downstairs rooms and managed to break it into pieces small enough to burn. He had just climbed the stairs with the wood tucked under his arm, and was about to reach out and open the door to his room when he heard a noise from the other side. Quickly he froze and listened.

There was a dull bumping noise then the sound of paper. Someone was in his room...maybe it was the person behind all these pranks. Either way Kaleb was determined to get to the bottom of this craziness. So raising a splintered chair leg as a weapon above his head he flung open the door and went charging into the room.

"GOTCHA!!" He cried as he did so. Then realized he was talking to an empty room. The only evidence that anything had been disturbed was the empty bread package that had contained his single slice of bread. So it's a hungry ghost Kaleb thought. There was a creak from behind him and Kaleb spun around just in time to see the corner of his wiener package vanishing around the doorframe out into the hall.

"OH NO YOU DON'T," Kaleb shouted as he threw all caution to the wind and leapt on the rapidly vanishing sausage packet. He managed to grab onto the very corner, and commenced a life and death struggle for his hot-dogs, but the small corner he had was slippery and after a moment it slipped from his grasp and disappeared around the corner.

Kaleb leapt to his feet and jumped out into the hallway just as a door at the far end of the hallway slammed shut. "QUICK," Kaleb said under his breath...squinting sideways at the door. "BUT NOT QUICK ENOUGH."

He hefted the chair leg in his hand and stalked down the corridor to the door. Carefully he turned the knob and went in. The room he was in was covered in white sheets, mirrors old and dusty hung from the walls and furniture sat disowned and forgotten.

Kaleb scanned the room before him. "Trust a ghost to hide in a room full of white sheets," he chided, as he made his way through the maze of covered chairs and tables. He was about halfway across the room when something suddenly erupted from under one of the tables on the far wall. Taking with it one of the flowing white sheets. Kaleb leapt after it but missed.

It scooted quickly out the door and down the stairs to the lobby. Kaleb ran after it only to slip on a discarded wiener halfway down the stairs and end up tumbling headfirst the rest of the way. Not beaten, he sprang nimbly back to his feet the instant he hit the lobby floor and peered around him. It doesn't want the wiener anymore...it was PERSONAL.

Meanwhile in the basement, Jacob was still chuckling and very proud of himself. He had managed to take the entire 10-meter length of old chain and draped himself in it without making a sound. In addition to this he had also hung several large tin pots about his neck. He had then opened the grate on the furnace, which lead up to the heat ducts, which ran through the entire house and made sure that the pipe ways were clear. This was going to be a night that city boy would not soon forget.

Kaleb crept silently down the hallway towards the kitchen. Stopping every couple of steps to listen. The wind whistled outside and a shutter banged somewhere upstairs. Wide scared eyes watched him from the heating duct in the wall. He kept on listening.

Downstairs, Jacob looked at his watch. On the stroke of 8pm all hell was going to break loose. He leaned in close to the open grate and counted quietly down.

5...4...3...2...

At exactly the stroke of 8, Jacob took a huge breath and howled for all he was worth up the furnace grate. Clanking and shaking his pots and chains against the floor or wall or whatever was closest. And he was completely correct.

All hell DID break loose. No sooner had he begun his hullabaloo when the very bowls of hell itself opened up and the wailing cries of tortured souls flooded down on him as well as a showering cloud of ash and soot. Completely unprepared for this as he was, Jacob BELLOWED and jumped back.

Unfortunately the chains in which he had draped himself became snagged on the furnace grate, and thinking that demonic hands had seized him he began to thrash and howl trying to free himself, and clear the soot from his eyes and mouth.

Kaleb as well was completely unprepared for the events that were about to unfold before him. Thinking that he had the thieving spirit cornered in the broom cupboard, he was advancing on it when suddenly from behind him, the grill exploded off the heating vent and a figure wrapped in a cloud of soot and white linen, rocketed out howling for all it was worth. Never one to miss an opportunity, and himself now seized by an unreasoning terror, Kaleb also yowled at the top of his lungs.

Soot and ash stung his eyes and nose and horrible clanking and moaning sounds shook the very walls of the house. Fearing the end. He ran....

Ahead of him he could just make out a ghostly figure running ahead of him and howling as loud as he was.

Scared beyond words...Jacob thrashed about. Eventually he managed to free himself from the grate, and wasting no time he began to clamber quickly back out the way he had come, now completely convinced that the angels of death themselves where at his heels. He was still halfway out the window when the basement door exploded open and in a flurry of grubby linen and flying arms and legs, two figures sprinted down the stairs and careened across the basement.

Not looking where they were going, both of them fled head long into the stack of packing crates that Jacob had climbed to gain his freedom from the hell pit. They hit the crates with a crash sending Jacob cannoning the rest of the way out the window. Kaleb fell and covered his head as crates rained down on him.

Then...there was silence.

Outside Jacob staggered across the carriageway crossing himself and mumbling every prayer he could remember.

This was a night he would not soon forget...that was for sure.

Back in the basement all was quiet. Kaleb lay on his back covered in boxes. He mentally checked himself...and as far as he could tell there was nothing broken. Tentatively he moved. Sitting up slowly he looked around at the chaos that surrounded him. He had no idea how it had all happened. But seemingly for the moment at least, it was over. Carefully he pulled himself to his feet and began dusting himself down. It was then that he saw the trembling pile of boxes in the corner and remembered the ghost.

"OK" he spoke in a quiet voice. "The games are over now...so why don't you just come out and show yourself?" He edged slowly towards the shivering crates.

"Look I promise not to call the police if you just give up all these childish pranks right now."

He stopped just short of the boxes. He could see under the pile, the sheet covered in soot and crumpled. Reaching out a cautious hand he carefully lifted away the top box. Wild scared eyes as big as dinner plates stared out at him and a fearful voice whined pathetically. Kaleb didn't know what to make of it so he kept digging. Removing another box revealed a head. The head of a man, shaking with terror.

Kaleb stood back. Hands on hips. "So I was right," he said accusingly. "It was all pranks."

The man looked at him. Still trembling.

"Well the games up. You might As well come out," he said. When the man didn't move he became angry.

"I said COME OUT!" He reached out to grab the man's shoulder, which instantly set him to howling almightily and trying desperately to dig his way deeper into the piles of boxes.

Kaleb stood back stunned, as the man cowered whimpering before him. What on Earth was going on here? It was then that Kaleb caught a glimmer of metal from around the man's neck. Looking closer he saw that it was a thin ragged looking collar...A DOG COLLAR!!

Pieces began to click into place.

"NO" he thought...."This is insane." He kicked himself for his own silly thoughts. Then leaned in closer. "What's your name?" He asked, again the trembling whimper.

Somewhere in the back of his mind he knew what was needed. But his logical side fought it. It was ridiculous. INSANE. But what else could be done? Sighing, he stretched out his hand and softly clicked his fingers. "PUP?" He said.

The man in the crates looked at him. Then titled his head quizzically to one side, just as a curious puppy might. That was the clincher. This man thought he was a dog. It was too bizarre. But then again he was verging on insanity himself right now...so did it really matter?

Kaleb snapped his fingers again, "Come pup," He said soothingly.

The man carefully stretched out his neck and sniffed at the air in front of

Kaleb.

"Here boy," Kaleb crooned sweetly, "Come on."

The man, still sniffing took a careful step forwards. Bowing his head he looked up at Kaleb and lightly sniffed at his hand. Kaleb noticed as the man moved forwards that besides the small concession of the collar, He seemed to be completely naked. Kaleb flushed for a second and looked away. No one at home was going to believe this. Then he felt a nose bump against his still outstretched hand.

He looked back and saw the man lightly nuzzling his fingers. Slowly so as not to scare him, Kaleb turned his hand palm out and the man placed his nose in Kaleb's hand.

"GOOD BOY," he sang, and found himself smiling as he gently ran his fingers over the man's face. Kaleb looked down and saw that a hastily scrawled tag hung from the collar. It read simply. "CHASE."

He said the word. "CHASE." The man reacted instantly, pricking up his head and panting. His eyes sparkled and a smile twitched at the edge of his mouth.

"Is that your name?" Kaleb asked, "CHASE?"

The man pooch became excited. Stomping his hands on the ground and whining. Kaleb stood and took a step back. He stopped and squatted down.

"HERE CHASE," he called holding out his arms wide.

Chase growled and now on all fours he turned in little circles. He seemed undecided. Uncertain. Kaleb called again. "It's OK boy...COME ON CHASE!" Suddenly the pooch seemed to give in....And in three lumbering steps he was across the floor and landing squarely in Kaleb's lap. They both fell back. Kaleb laughing and Chase ARRFING for all he was worth. Chase sat on Kaleb's chest pinning him down and slobbering his wet tongue over Kaleb's face. And laughing Kaleb tried to fend him off.

"Well"...Kaleb thought to himself as he ruff patted the pooches head. "If this is being crazy...maybe the sane people are missing out."

An hour later Kaleb sat in a large over stuffed chair in the library, Chase squatted on all fours on the rug in front of him. Kaleb picked out another chunk of the remaining wiener and held it up.

"Here ya go," he smiled.

Chase launched himself up and snatched the sausage from Kaleb's hand. "GOOD BOY" Kaleb approved. He sat back in the chair and Chase trotted over and laid his head in Kaleb's lap looking up at him.

Kaleb stroked Chase's chin thinking. "You certainly are a mystery aren't you" he whispered.

"I wonder if I will ever know your story."

As he was saying this...The long day and the warm fire did their work. And before he knew it he was slipping down into a solid dreamless sleep.

No terrors, no demons...just peaceful sleep.

A distant almost heard noise woke Kaleb from his sleep. He rolled over and stretched. A quick glance at his watch told him it was 10 minutes past midnight. Slowly he sat up and looked around the room. Aside from his few belongings it was empty.

"Chase"? He called softly.

There was no reply. Kaleb climbed out of the chair and went to the door. He opened it and stuck his head out into the hallway, "Here boy," he called looking left and right.

The night seemed unnaturally still. There was not a breath of wind and Kaleb's breath was fogging into frosty clouds in front of him. Pulling his quilt tight about him he stepped out into the hallway. It was then that he noticed that the sounds his feet made hitting the floor boards sounded dulled and far away. There seemed to him to be some kind of veil, like an ethereal blanket cast over the house. He stepped slowly out into the hallway and pulled the door closed behind him. It made a dull clunk as the latch caught and held. As Kaleb moved down the steps he felt as though he were moving through a still life photograph.

ABSOLUTELY nothing moved or made a sound.

Half way down the stairs he heard a noise, from the back yard, a high-pitched bark. It echoed down the hall in slow motion. Kaleb turned and headed across the lobby. The faster he moved the slower he went. It felt like swimming through cobwebs. Eventually he reached the kitchen door and went through.

The kitchen lay in silence and Kaleb strode through calling out as he went. "CHASE Here. What are ya up to mutt?"

He stepped up and opened the back door. Silently it relented and swung away from him. There was a small step down onto the back porch where stood old broken plant pots and a ruined porch swing. Kaleb looked out across the yard, and almost gasped at the vision before him.

The garden path lead out into the yard, winding it's way between long disused garden beds that now harbored little more than clumps of tangled weed and grass. Here and there a broken stepping-stone was the only sign that a cobbled path had ever existed. The moon hung full and round in the sky. Bathing everything beneath it in a soft gossamer shawl of pearl colored light. But by far, the most striking part of this whole scene was taking place in the long twisted shadows that snaked out from the over hanging branches of a long dead shade tree. For beneath these branches stood Chase, on all fours barking happily. And before him stood a spectral image, like a vision, a tall man, with very familiar features stood before Chase laughing and waving a stick.

The man seemed almost to be made of crystal or a strange kind of solid smoke, as Kaleb could see directly through his glowing transparent form. All around him a silent breeze seemed to carrying curling tendrils of fine white mist like a cloak wafting endlessly about him. Kaleb felt the air from the backyard and shivered. There was no doubt in his mind that Kaleb was looking at Preston Wainwright, the man from the painting above the fireplace.

Chase pounced forwards then back. Barking happily as Preston waved the stick teasing him and pretending to throw it. Then suddenly he pulled back his arm and let it fly. It arced through the air, landing with a soft thud directly at Kaleb's feet. It lay there unnoticed as Kaleb continued to stare at the ghostly visage before him.

Chase bounded up and picked up the stick in his mouth. Missing Kaleb for a moment then suddenly seeing him in the shadows and stopping. The stick fell to the ground and Chase froze. Looking first from Preston then to Kaleb.

Preston suddenly saw Kaleb at the edge of the porch and his smile faded. His face seemed to take on the hollow drawn expression of a truly tortured soul.

"I don't believe it," Kaleb whispered, still in shock. "I don't think I can take much more of this."

Chase, forgetting the stick, quickly scooted back to Preston and sat beside him. Preston said nothing. He simply watched. Kaleb took a faltering step forwards. Almost in a trance he staggered through the garden beds, never once taking his eyes from Preston. He stopped when he was no more than two meters from them and breathed deeply.

"I don't believe it," he repeated.

Preston looked at Kaleb. "My name is Preston Wainright," he offered.

"Yes" Kaleb said still unblinking. "I know."

Slowly he reached out a hand and held it in front of himself. Preston carefully reached out his own hand and lightly touched his smoky index finger to Kaleb's outstretched palm. Kaleb thought that it felt very much like the fluttering of butterfly's wings. It was solid. Not translucent like the movies would have you believe. It had shape and form and solidity.

"Are you a ghost?" Kaleb asked.

"Yes" Preston replied smiling. "I died 6 years ago."

Kaleb blinked and looked down at Chase. "And you knew about him?" He asked the pooch.

Chase whined pitifully and covered his eyes with a paw.

"Don't blame him," Preston said, "In life we were...Together. He and I were soul mates. Dog and master. But my life was brought up short by an illness that no one had seen coming. I did my best to allow for him after I was gone but some very bad choices have made it very difficult."

'Choices?" Kaleb asked.

"Yes. The people that I had organized to look after Chase turned out to be, how shall we say, less than helpful."

"So is that why you stayed then? I mean here on Earth with us mortals?" "Yes" Preston answered. "You see...Chase is my unfinished business...until he is safe and cared for I can't move on." Preston crouched down and scratched Chase on the back of the neck.

"That doesn't seem fair" Kaleb said.

Preston looked up at Kaleb and smiled. "Fair or not I would have it no other way."

"So why don't you just FIND somebody else?" Kaleb inquired.

"I have been looking but I can only do so much," Preston sighed.

"The initial spark must come from Chase and the person. You see my job is not to let him go. But to help him let go."

Kaleb suddenly understood. "So you are looking for another soul mate for Chase then. Not just another Owner?"

Preston smiled, "Exactly."

Kaleb was still dazed. But Preston's words were making a kind of sense to him. If what he was saying was true, then it was probably one of the most selfless acts in recorded history. An act fuelled by true love. The truest love that Kaleb had ever encountered.

Without really understanding why Kaleb, suddenly crouched down and looked Chase directly in the eyes, "You are a very lucky pooch ya know that?" He scratched Chase under the chin and Chase licked Kaleb on the face. Slobbering over his nose. Kaleb chuckled and Preston smiled.

"He seems to like you."

Kaleb stood and turned to Preston, "So who was the person that you had organized to look after him then?"

"A very un-saintly man," Preston frowned. "He used to work here as a grounds keeper."

"OH DON'T TELL ME," Kaleb suddenly interjected.

"Short little ugly guy with a scar on his cheek? Goes by the name of Morrison? Jacob Morrison?"

"Yes...regrettably," Preston sighed. "He seemed like the most obvious person for the job. Until I died. Ever since, he has done nothing but neglect Chase and bury himself in the search for the will."

"The will?" Kaleb asked, "There is a will wrapped up in this somewhere as well?"

"Before I died," Preston explained, "I signed everything I owned, including the house and all my money, to Chase. However since Chase is not as we would say naturally human, there were problems. And since a suitable replacement for me could not be found I entrusted the Will to Chase to hide. Morrison soon got wind of the will's existence and forewent his duties as Chase's guardian to look for it. He however does not know that Chase is the only one who knows where the will is."

Kaleb looked confused, "So why don't you just get Chase to go fetch the Will and hand everything over to him. There must be enough money in it to see that he is taken care of until another YOU comes along?"

"That was my original planning". Preston agreed. "But there in lies the problem."

"I don't understand" Kaleb said.

Preston raised a transparent finger...."Watch."

He turned to Chase who had been watching all intently and idly scratching fleas.

"Chase," Preston said, "Where's the will?" Chase instantly pricked up his ears and stood up on all fours.

"Get the will" Preston urged him, "Go on boy, GET IT."

Chase almost immediately set up a mournful howling and began waving both paws in the air in front of him.

"What's he doing?" Kaleb asked.

"That's the sign that I taught him for HUGGY his chew toy," Preston explained, "So I can only deduce from that, that he has hidden the will in HUGGY."

"OK so lets go get HUGGY," Kaleb said becoming more and more confused by the minute.

"Again the problem," Preston replied. Turning back to Chase he spoke again, "Where's HUGGY Chase?"

Chase tilted his head to the side.

"GET HUGGY...GO ON" Preston practically begged.

Again Chase began to Howl almightily and ran trembling behind Kaleb's legs.

"OK so now what's up?" Kaleb asked leaning down and gently stroking Chase on the back.

"That's just it," Preston sighed, "I don't know, it's almost as if he is too afraid to go get HUGGY."

"Jeez," Kaleb whistled, "must be one hell of a scary chew toy then."

Preston raised an eyebrow at Kaleb. "Actually it's a small brown teddy bear, with jointed arms and legs...probably missing an eye."

Kaleb suddenly stood up, "ABOUT THIS BIG?" He held out his hands in front of him to indicate the size he meant.

"Yes why?" Preston asked, suddenly very eager.

"Well," Kaleb said "I know why he doesn't want to go get it."

"Why?" Preston asked.

"Because it's in Jacob's shed at the bottom of the grounds."

_____

Preston looked at Kaleb. Chase looked at Kaleb.

"OOOOOOH NO!!!!" Kaleb exclaimed backing away. "Definitely not."

He knew what was coming and he wanted no part of it.

"Please," Preston implored. "You are the only hope Chase has."

To emphasize the point Chase tilted his head to one side and whined softly. Kaleb got the decided feeling that he was being double-teamed.

"That old Geezer is NUTS!" He protested, " If he finds me in his shed he is just as likely to pepper my butt with shotgun lead."

"It will only take a moment," Preston urged.

"NO!"

"And Chase can keep watch."

"NO!"

"You will be in and out before he even knows you have been there."
"NO." Kaleb said stubbornly, "NO...NO...NO!"

"I am going to go back into the house, pack the rest of my gear, and come morning I am gonna be well on my way to hiking outta this crazy place." Preston looked beaten. "Then all is lost," his shoulders drooped.

Chase flopped down on the ground and HUMPHED loudly.

"It's been a real BANG guys but I gotta be goin'," Kaleb turned to go, then looked back over his shoulder. "And besides, you need a brave guy, you can do way better than me."

Then turning, he walked slowly back towards the house. Climbing the steps he went into the kitchen and shut the door behind him. Almost simultaneously the door clicked shut, and the still night air was wracked with a pitiful howl.

"Coward" Kaleb whispered under his breath.

The next morning Kaleb moved quickly about the bedroom packing his things.

"Where did I put my torch?" He wondered to himself out loud.

Turning he saw Chase sitting in the doorway with his flashlight in his mouth.

"NO." He said again.

Chase growled. Then jumping up he started running in tiny circles around Kaleb's feet barking wildly.

"AND THROWING A TEMPER TANTRUM WILL NOT HELP YOU!!" Kaleb shouted over the din.

Chase stopped and looked up at Kaleb.

Kaleb knelt down and looked the pooch squarely in the eye. "You gotta understand," He tried to explain.

"I got a job...I have to get back to it...and a home...and there are bills to pay...I can't just run off...and..."

He stopped. "LOOK AT ME, I am explaining why I am a coward to a DOG!" Then he took a step back, "DOUBLE LOOK AT ME...I am explaining why I am a coward to a man who thinks he is a dog, that I think is a dog...but is really a man."

He sat down on the side of the bed. "I think I'm losing it."

Chase trotted over and plunked his head in Kaleb's lap.

"And you're not helping," Kaleb sighed, patting Chase on the back of the neck.

An hour later Kaleb stood at the front steps of the house. He had his backpack on, and was looking at Chase, who was standing on the porch steps. "Well," he said, "I guess this is it pooch." He held out his hand, Chase stayed on the steps whining softly.

Kaleb looked sad. "OK," he said. "I guess I will see ya then."

Hitching his pack higher onto his back he turned and started away down the driveway. "Stubborn dog" he grumbled under his breath. At the bottom of the drive near the gate, Kaleb met Jacob coming up the drive...a shotgun still steaming under one arm and a brace of foul, dead and dripping blood, under the other. Jacob stopped directly in front of him.

"Leaving then are ya?" He inquired, squinting at Kaleb.

"Umm...yeah I guess so," Kaleb answered.

"The house not what you were expecting was it?" Jacob's sneering mouth almost smiled.

"No, not really." Kaleb replied, "I was looking for something with..." he faltered. Lost for words. He could feel Jacob's eyes burrowing into him.

"WITH?" The wrinkled old man asked. Leaning slightly closer.
"With less pets" Kaleb blurted out...then instantly regretted his words.

"AAAAHHH so you met that mange ridden dog then did ya?"

Kaleb was taken aback. "Yeah I did. He can be very loud when he wants to be."

Jacob chuckled evilly. "Not to worry." He said cracking the barrel of his shotgun and placing another two shells in the chamber. "That won't be a problem for much longer."

Kaleb's blood ran cold.

"OH" he laughed nervously. "Good to hear it...that mangy mutt deserves everything he gets."

Jacob leaned in close to Kaleb so they were mere inches apart. "Folks always gets what's comin' to 'em," he grinned, through yellow broken teeth.

"Well"...Kaleb said. "It's getting late, I gotta be going."

Jacob tilted his hat. "You be careful," he said. "These woods can be mighty dangerous to them what don't know their way."

"Thanks I will," Kaleb said, backing hastily away. "BYE." Quickly he turned, and almost ran the short distance to the fence and clambered through.

Jacob watched him go then turned back up the drive. "Now for that dog," he growled spitting in the gravel. Slowly he began to clump his way up the trail to the house.

Jacob stood puffing at the foot of the porch stairs. Mopping his brow with a grubby handkerchief he stomped up the stairs and flung open the front door. The house inside was quiet. Slowly he moved across the lobby, blinking to adjust his eyes to the darkness.

"Hey poochy," He called in a gravelly voice. "Old Jacob is here," he hefted the shotgun in his hands, and mounted the main staircase. The stairs creaked as he climbed them one at a time, and tiny puffs of dust curled up from the carpet under his boots. At the top of the stairs he turned and looked up and down the hallway. Then stepping quietly as his bulky form would allow, he moved over to the door directly in front of him and pushed it open.

"Here poochy" he called looking about the room.

In the corner of the room, under a table draped with a white cloth, Kaleb held his breath and clamped his hand down harder over Chase's mouth. His heart was still pounding from his run back up the hill to the house. He had arrived only seconds before Jacob, and had only just managed to drag Chase under the table before Jacob had come in. Now the confused puppy whined under Kaleb's hand as Jacob's heavy foot prints clumped about the room. Kaleb prayed to every god that he could think of. After what seemed like an eternity, Jacob, satisfied that the room was empty, left and went on to the next room.

Kaleb put up his finger to his lips in front of Chase. "SSSSSH," he whispered. "Quiet boy."

Chase, understanding that something was amiss, stayed silent.

After searching through half a dozen more rooms Jacob once again descended to the lobby. "No matter pooch," he called into the empty house. "There's plenty of time, and Old Jacob is a patient man." Having said that, he pulled the door shut behind him, and shuffled off, back across the carriageway.

Kaleb watched him go from the second story window. When he was out of sight, Kaleb ran down the stairs to the lobby.

"PRESTON!!" He bellowed at the ceiling. "PRESTON WE HAVE GOT TO TALK!!"

"No need to shout" Came a voice from behind him.

Kaleb spun and saw Preston had appeared, and was drifting slightly off the floor. "I am never far away," he smiled.

"Preston...thank god," Kaleb exclaimed. "This is getting dangerous, I just met Jacob on the path and he didn't say as much, but he made it quite clear to me that Chase is a problem he intends to get rid of no matter what. I only just got back here in time. If I hadn't who knows what would have happened if Jacob had found Chase."

Preston looked slightly surprised. "Well thank you Kaleb," he said. "What do you propose we do then?" He looked hard into Kaleb's eyes.

Kaleb paused for a moment. "Well," he said. "I propose we go get ourselves a TEDDY BEAR!!!!!!"

Preston grinned "AGREED!" He said.

Chase scratched a flea.

The stick of dynamite turned gracefully in the air twice then landed with a soft slap back in Jacob's hand. He rolled it lightly between thumb and forefinger and grinned a crooked grin. Carefully he placed the stick back in the box with its 19 other friends.

"If I can't have the house and the money," he hissed under his breath. "Then I will see to it that no one else can either." Chuckling to himself he placed a large coil of fuse in the box with the dynamite, then picking it up, he tucked the box under his arm. Things were certainly about to go off with a bang.

Fifteen minutes later Kaleb and Chase crawled to the edge of the clearing and peered out from between the fern fronds.

"It looks clear," Kaleb whispered surveying the broken down old shack and the tiny yard around it. Chase sniffed at the air and whined softly.

"I know you don't like it here boy," Kaleb said, ruff patting the pooch on the back of the neck. "But it's the only way." He looked at Chase and sighed. "Believe me," he said reassuringly. "If there were any other way I would take it"

Chase leant his head against Kaleb's shoulder and whined again.

"Well," Kaleb said, "I guess now is as good a time as any."

He took hold of Chase's chin and looked at him seriously. "Now you remember what I said right boy?" He said.

Chase barked and stomped his front paws on the soft leafy ground.

"Good boy" Kaleb said. "I am counting on you to warn me if anything happens while I am inside ok?"

Again Chase barked.

"OK now Guard," Kaleb stood, and crossed the clearing to the hut. When he got to the door he turned back and looked at Chase. "GUARD BOY," he called in a low whisper.

Chase sat up as tall as he could and thrust out his chest proudly looking back and forth. A serious frown creased his brow. Kaleb smiled and quickly slipped into the hut closing the door behind him.

Inside the hut was almost exactly as Kaleb had seen it earlier. He crossed quickly to the mantle and took down the ragged bear. Turning it over in his hands he saw a tiny corner of paper protruding from the back seam of the bear. That was enough to convince Kaleb that he had the right bear. He could check the contents properly when he was somewhere safer. Turning, he started to pick his way back through the junk strewn about. Passing the bed he stepped over a broken chair and his foot came down slightly wrong. He staggered and tripped landing on a wooden crate.

Outside Chase looked around him. He was alone and the forest, even in the daytime was a dark scary place. He shivered slightly but did not move. He had been ordered to Guard, and Guard he would. There was the sudden soft sound of a snapping twig and Chase cocked his head. Listening intently. He sniffed at the air, a scent. Too faint to recognize but not quite right either. He stood up on all fours and peered through the underbrush in the direction the noise had come from. The tall green fern fronds swayed in the slight chill breeze, but nothing else...then again...SNAP. This time Chase heard it distinctly.

He took a cautious step forwards still sniffing at the air. Then came a rustling directly ahead of him. He lowered his head and growled low and menacing. He took three more steps forward. He was undecided. Should he stay and guard or should he explore the noise? Two more steps and he was closer to the place the noise had come from. Suddenly the barrel of a shotgun poked out from the bushes and stopped an inch from the tip of Chase's nose.

"Well, well, well," came the grating of an all too familiar voice. "Looks like I caught me a puppy."

Chase's blood ran cold and he whined miserably.

Kaleb burst from the hut calling for Chase.

"Chase, come here boy we gotta go," he said clutching a wooden crate that had the word DYNAMITE printed on the side. "I found this in the hut. I know what that crazy old coot is...up...to."

Kaleb stopped in his tracks as he saw Chase cowering at the edge of the clearing and Jacob standing over him with the barrel of his shotgun against the dog's temple.

"Crazy old coot then is it?" Jacob growled, leering sidelong at Kaleb. Kaleb's mind was racing. What should he do? He could throw the box in hopes of knocking the gun from Jacob's hand. But that would put Chase in more danger than he was ready to put him in. He could jump on Jacob, and wrestle him down. Probably with the same result to Chase. No matter which way Kaleb looked at it Jacob had the upper hand.

Kaleb licked his lips. "Easy Jacob," he said soothingly. "Let's not do anything silly now."

Chase whined and Jacob nudged him with the gun barrel.

"SHUT UP DOG!" He hissed between his teeth.

Kaleb stepped forwards, and Jacob cocked the gun. "Any closer and he's dead," he warned "And believe me, after all the trouble this MUTT has caused me. It would be a pleasure to send him on to his owner."

Kaleb flared with rage.

"Now," Jacob said, "Perhaps you would like to tell me just what it was you were after in my hut?"

Kaleb shrugged. "Nothing." He said. "Just naturally inquisitive I guess."
Jacob nudged Chase again with the gun.

"Ok," Kaleb said. "I was looking for this," he held out HUGGY.

Chase saw HUGGY and began to twitch and whine. Jacob glared at the teddy bear in Kaleb's hand. Kaleb could see the old man thinking.

"Yeah," Kaleb continued, trying to hold Jacob's attention. "I saw a picture of Chase playing with it and I thought it might help settle him down."

Jacob turned his gaze back on Kaleb. "Give it to me," he said holding out his free hand.

Kaleb paused for a moment.

Jacob pushed the gun barrel hard into Chase's temple. "GIVE IT TO ME!!!!"

Kaleb shrugged. "OK...ok...here...CATCH!!!" Pulling back his arm, Kaleb launched the bear into the air. It arced gracefully up, then began to descend towards Jacob. Momentarily he was distracted and reached out to catch the flying toy. In that instant, a blinding flash of light erupted between Kaleb and Jacob like a thousand flash bulbs going off simultaneously.

A roaring wind exploded from nowhere and leaves and debris were blown in every direction. Jacob bellowed and covered his eyes to shield them from the blinding light. Chase howled and cowered low to the ground and Kaleb staggered back stunned. As the light ebbed and pulsed before him and the wind roared in his ears, Jacob heard a thundering voice. Rumbling like a clap of thunder. "GREETINGS JACOB," Preston said. Jacob squinted into the light. He could only just make out the shimmering outline of a man. A man he knew all too well.

"PRESTON!" He gasped.

Preston hovered before him, haloed in a shroud of raging light and wind like the visage of an avenging angel. The surrounding forest was lit like daylight.

"I HAVE BEEN WATCHING YOU JACOB!!" Preston boomed. "LEAVE HERE NOW!!!"

Stunned as he was, Jacob's greed shone through his fear. "NOOOO" He yelled. "IT'S MINE!!!"

He raised the shotgun and loosed both barrels into the light ahead of him. Both shots went straight through and exploded into a tree on the other side above Kaleb's head sending splintered wood and sawdust raining down on him. Terrified, Chase could stand no more. Yelping at the top of his lungs, he jumped up onto all fours and sprinted away through the underbrush.

"CHASE" Kaleb called after him.

But Chase was far too scared to hear. His only instinct was to run. Kaleb staggered to his feet and followed. The wind buffeted him and he only just managed to keep his feet under him. Somewhere behind he thought he could hear the sound of something crashing through the underbrush behind him. He didn't look. He just kept running.

Scant moments later Kaleb burst out of the trees, He was back at the house. Wasting no time he sprinted gasping across the drive. The front door banged in the wind. Kaleb went in. The house was dark and silent. "CHASE" he called. "HERE BOY!"

There was no reply. Instinctively Kaleb mounted the stairs. "Chase we gotta go boy it's not safe here."

From the top of the stairs Kaleb heard pitiful whining. He took the last four steps in one stride and there, cowering against the far wall of the hall was Chase. Trembling with fear. Pressed as hard as he could against the wall. "Chase c'mere boy," Kaleb called desperately trying to sound as solid and reassuring as he could, but inwardly he wanted to curl up and howl himself.

"It's OK boy. Come on we gotta go now".

Kaleb held out his hand for Chase to come. Still trembling Chase sniffed the air.

In the lobby Jacob stood heaving for breath in the front doorway.

He could see Kaleb crouched at the top of the stairs. Rage flared inside him and he leveled the shotgun, Just as he squeezed the trigger a gust of wind came from nowhere and sent the front door slamming into his back. The shots went wild, exploding into the chandelier, making it rock and swing crazily. Kaleb threw himself forwards and covered his head as shattered shards of crystal rained down. Chase howled and scampered to the other end of the hall. Kaleb rolled over and looked down into the lobby. Jacob stood in the dim light reloading his shotgun. Fear gave Kaleb wings and he was up like a shot and running after Chase. In the shadowy light of the hallway Kaleb saw Chase's bare behind vanishing through a tiny doorway and up a narrow flight of stairs.

He followed.

Down below Jacob turned the detonator over in his hands. It was a new fangled remote type. No wires to worry about. Reason had long since fled his mind. All that mattered now was the dog. He had to get the dog. Spitting on the floor he slowly began to clump his way up the stairs. As long as they continued up he would get them. Once they got to the top there was nowhere else to go.

The attic was a small dingy room right in the top of the house. It was packed with broken furniture and bric-a-brac. A small arched window on the far wall let beams of dust-faded light in, casting long thin shadows over the piled contents of the room. Dust ebbed slowly in sluggish clouds and Kaleb was assailed by the gathered must of years.

"Chase," he called into the darkness.

A quiet whimper was his only reply. Away down the stairs Kaleb could hear clumping feet. Jacob was going to find them. Kaleb threw caution to the wind and began pitching junk over his shoulder. If the dog wouldn't come to HIM, then HE would go to the dog. Wedging a chair under the door handle to keep Jacob out as long as he could Kaleb rifled through the oddments.

Jacob stopped at the door and turned the handle. Something on the other side blocked it from opening. He grinned a crooked yellow grin and raised the barrel of the shotgun. There was an ear splitting explosion and the door disintegrated into dust. Jacob strode into the room just in time to see Kaleb's feet vanishing out the attic window.

"DAMN YOU HOLD STILL" he bellowed.

Out on the roof, Kaleb was almost dragging Chase by the collar.

"If there was any time in the universe to be a stubborn dog Chase, THIS IS NOT IT!"

He stopped and looked at the terrified pooch. "PLEASE" he said. "How can I make you understand?"

He crouched down and took Chase's head in his hands. "If we don't get away from here we are going to DIE!!"

There came the sound of crashing furniture from the attic as Jacob waded through the rubbish to the window. Kaleb stood and skull dragged Chase over the crest of the roof to the relative but all too fleeting safety of the other side. Kaleb heard a crash of glass and knew they didn't have long.

In a last ditch effort, Kaleb called to the sky. "PRESTON PLEASE...WE NEED YOUR HELP."

A second later the ghostly image of Preston appeared on the roof before them. Chase instantly galloped across the loose tiles and sat rubbing his head against Preston's leg and whining. Preston looked at Kaleb then down at Chase. He squatted down on his haunches and spoke to the terrified dog.

"Chase," he said. "You have to be a good boy."

Chase tilted his head to the side and looked into Preston's eyes.

"Kaleb is trying to help you," Preston continued, "he is a good man. You must be a good boy for him."

Kaleb thought he heard Preston's voice crack slightly. Chase howled and pushed himself against Preston's chest.

"You must go with him now."

Preston hugged Chase around the neck and stood up. "Go with Kaleb" he said quietly.

Chase turned and looked at Kaleb and as he did Preston slowly faded into mist and was gone. When he looked back Chase saw that besides Kaleb and himself the roof was empty. Instantly he began to howl mournfully. Then he stopped.

Although tears were streaming down his face Kaleb put out his hand. "HERE BOY" he called.

Chase paused for a moment. Then trotting slowly over to Kaleb he placed his head in Kaleb's hand and nuzzled his palm. It was that instant that Jacob crested the roof top. Kaleb stood and moved in front of Chase, who crouched low and growled deep in his chest.

"Give me the dog and I will let you go," Jacob offered.

Kaleb stood his ground. He looked at Jacob and saw that HUGGY was stuffed into the top of his belt.

"LOOK!" Kaleb said. "Why don't you just take the deed for the house and let us both go, it's hidden in the back of the bear."

Jacob laughed. "You honestly expect me to believe that city boy?" He chuckled.

"It's true" Kaleb protested. "LOOK FOR YOURSELF!!"

Jacob faltered, then holding the detonator up so Kaleb could see it he said, "Be warned city boy. A flick of the wrist and we all go to hell."

Kaleb stood frozen as Jacob pulled the ragged bear from his belt. Using one hand he turned it over and looked. There was the corner of paper. He pulled on it slightly and revealed the word DEED.

Almost insanely he began to laugh. "I had it in my shed the WHOLE TIME!" He guffawed.

Kaleb looked down at Chase who was still growling at Jacob. "Chase," he whispered. Chase looked at him.

"Where's HUGGY?" Kaleb hissed.

Chase cocked his head and looked confused.

"Where's HUGGY Chase?" Kaleb repeated. He motioned with his hand towards Jacob.

Chase looked at Jacob and saw the bear in his hand. He looked quickly back at Kaleb understanding sparkled in his eyes.

"Get HUGGY boy," Chase whispered. "Go get him."

Jacob was still laughing when Chase launched himself and landed squarely on his chest. The force sent them both crashing backwards. The detonator flew from Jacob's hand. It spun through the air. Kaleb saw it and lunged. He slid along the roof with hands outstretched and the detonator landed an inch from his fingertips. It jarred solidly and the green active light suddenly blinked to red.

The display showed a count down of 5. Kaleb picked up the detonator and sprinted across the roof.

"CHASE GET DOWN!!" He yelled.

He threw himself bodily onto Chase and covered him.

In the basement of the house, a tiny spark flashed blue in the darkness. The fuse ignited, and 5 seconds later the box of dynamite erupted into a dazzling ball of flame. The explosion erupted up through the house like a fountaining volcano of flame taking with it anything in its way. Windows exploded and support beams groaned and gave way. The entire house rocked violently from the force of the blast.

On the roof all hell was breaking loose. Jacob staggered to his feet and bent to pick up his shotgun just as a section of the roof erupted and a searing tongue of white-yellow flame licked out. Jacob screamed and fell back clutching his hand. The roof trembled and began to crack apart as the entire house lurched sideways. Kaleb saw HUGGY lying on the roof and stood up. He staggered and almost lost his footing but managed to stay upright. There was another explosion from below and a hole opened under Kaleb's feet. He felt himself falling into the blazing pit below. Then suddenly he stopped.

He swung freely over the burning interior of the house. Looking up he saw that Chase had only just managed to grab the neck of his shirt in his teeth before he plunged to his doom. The straining pooch now stood balanced precariously on the edge of the crumbling roof trying desperately to drag Kaleb back to safety. Kaleb quickly reached up and grabbed on to the edge of the hole. And with the combined strength of himself and Chase managed to scramble his way back onto the roof. Jacob was nowhere to be seen, but to Kaleb at that instant, it was a very small worry.

"QUICK CHASE. We gotta be going," he called out. Chase was right by his side. They made their way back across the remains of the roof to the attic window. It was burning and inaccessible. Kaleb looked around frantically, he saw that the old dead tree that had stood by the house has been somewhat uprooted and now leaned against the eastern wall. Quickly Kaleb lead Chase over and eased him down onto the trunk of the tree. It was steep, but manageable. Kaleb was just clambering onto the trunk himself when a gunshot slammed into the tree beside his head. Looking up he saw Jacob. Bruised and bloodied, standing on the crest of the roof, his shotgun held wavering in his hands.

"GIVE ME THE DOG!!" He yelled over the crackling inferno.

Kaleb saw red. Looking around he picked up a large chunk of tree branch that lay on the roof beside him and stood up. "You just don't know when to give up do you?" He shouted crazily. Bracing himself he hefted the branch in his hands.

"YOU'RE NOT GETTING THE DOG...AND I...HAVE HAD...ENOUGH!!!!!!!" With that he bellowed insanely and sprinted across the roof.

Stunned Jacob raised his gun and fired. The shot grazed Kaleb on the shoulder and blood sprayed from a gaping wound. He staggered slightly but kept running. Holding the branch like a spear he lunged at Jacob. There was the sickening sound of tearing flesh and Jacob dropped his gun. Kaleb stood panting for a moment as Jacob looked at him stunned. Then slowly he stepped back. Looking down he saw the tree branch protruding from his chest at an odd angle. Disbelievingly he looked at Kaleb as a tiny trickle of blood ran down the side of his mouth. Then, without a sound he pitched backwards falling headlong into the burning abyss below.

Kaleb watched the flames engulf him, then clutching his arm he turned and staggered back to the tree.

Moments later Kaleb and Chase both stood watching the husk of the burnt out house collapse in on itself. Like a dying monster the old timbers groaned and screamed as they succumbed to the incredible heat. Pluming clouds of smoke and amber sparks drifted up in a twisting column from the ruined building. Kaleb put his hand on Chase's head and Chase nuzzled in close.

The next morning Kaleb woke with a start. Instantly he looked around for Chase. After the fire, they had both staggered back down the drive to Kaleb's car where they had collapsed exhausted, and slept. It was still very early. All around was shrouded in the steel gray light before dawn and a heavy blanket of fog hung everywhere. Kaleb heard Chase YAP excitedly and looked out behind the car. There he saw Chase. Kneeling in the wet grass. Preston stood beside him patting his head. Kaleb wrapped the car blanket around him and clambered out into the chill morning air.

Preston looked up and smiled as Kaleb approached. "Good morning." He grinned.

"I thought you were gone," Kaleb said, bewildered, "last night on the roof."

Preston smiled, "I couldn't let you leave without this," he pointed at Chase.

The pooch sat shaking a ragged teddy bear back and forth in his mouth. "I had the feeling it might come in handy."

Kaleb smiled, "Thank-you," he said. "For your help last night."

Preston said nothing.

"So what happens now?" Kaleb asked.

"My business here is finished." Preston replied, "I can go on to where I am supposed to be."

"And....what about Chase?" Kaleb looked down at the pooch.

"I was really hoping you could answer that for me," Preston said. "Especially after all the work I have done to get you here."

Kaleb looked up, a little shocked. "How do you mean?" He asked.

Preston smiled then spoke, "Sorry mister," he said in a tired voice. "The earliest we can do it will be tomorrow lunchtime."

Kaleb looked disbelievingly at the Ghost. "That was you?"
Preston chuckled "Yes of course it was...I had to keep you here somehow."

"So I was waiting for nothing?" Kaleb said half to himself. "The tow truck was never gonna show."

"Sorry," Preston apologized still smiling.

Kaleb suddenly looked up. "And I'll bet MY newspaper was the only paper with a for sale advertisement for this house in it too, wasn't it?"

Preston nodded.

Kaleb didn't know weather to yell or cry...So he laughed instead.

"So what do you say?" Preston asked seriously.

Kaleb thought hard.

"I don't know?" He replied, "I only have a small place...and he would be at home by himself while I was at work."

Chase trotted over to where Kaleb was standing and dropped HUGGY at his feet. He lowered his outstretched hand and Chase nuzzled into his palm.

The decision was made.

"And they say a DOG is a man's best friend huh?" Kaleb smiled. He squatted down onto his haunches and patted Chase on the head. Chase responded by licking Kaleb's face. Preston knelt beside them and looked at Chase.

"Ok boy," he said. "I have to go now," he put his arm around Chase and hugged him close. "I want you to be good for Kaleb and protect him well OK?"

Chase looked up at Kaleb and whined. Kaleb felt tears welling in his eyes again.

"No matter..." Preston's voice broke and he stopped and took a breath. "No matter where you go, if you ever need me I will be around ok pooch?" Chase nuzzled his snout hard into Preston's chest. Leaning on him as though that would stop him going.

Preston looked at Kaleb. "You have to promise me that you will care for Chase," he said.

Kaleb nodded. The knot in his throat made it impossible for him to speak. "Just remember there is no wrath like that of an avenging angel," Preston smiled.

Kaleb could just see a silvery tear trickling down his cheek.

Preston went to stand but Chase howled pitifully and leaned into him harder trying to clamber onto him.

"No pooch" Preston said. "I have to go now."

Tears streamed freely down Kaleb's cheeks as he watched the spectral figure stand and step back. Chase howled and beat his paws on the ground.

Preston looked directly into Kaleb's eyes. "Thank you" he said.

Kaleb knew then that the force of those words would travel with him throughout his life. Chase moved forwards and leaned in against Preston's leg whining softly.

Preston looked up at Kaleb. "You know what to do," was all he said.

Almost sobbing Kaleb knelt down and put out his hand. "Here boy," he called in a faltering voice, "Come here."

Chase wailed sorrowfully and moved behind Preston nuzzling his nose into the back of his knees.

Kaleb called again, "Chase...come on."

The words caught in his throat and he almost had to bodily push them out. Chase looked at Kaleb. His face torn with emotion. He looked first at Kaleb then at Preston. Pleading.

Preston pointed to Kaleb..."Go on boy," he said.

Chase looked at him for a moment...then...slowly he stood, and walked sadly over to where Kaleb knelt waiting. Kaleb wrapped him arms around the heart broken pooch and hugged him close. Lightly Chase turned his face to Kaleb's and slowly licked his cheek.

Preston smiled, "Be well," he said. Then as Kaleb and Chase watched, a shimmering aura of blue and white light grew from nowhere and enveloped Preston.

It flowed around him like a shroud of purity. Its brightness was blinding. Sparkling fingers of light danced around him like playing children.

Kaleb was suddenly swamped in a wave of warmth.

"Goodbye," Preston called from within the cloud. Then suddenly it exploded, erupting into a billion tiny sparks that floated out and slowly faded into nothingness.

Chase watched the last tiny spark fall at his feet and fade into the damp soil in front of him.

Preston was gone.

They stood in silence for a long while, not moving.

Then, still wiping tears from his eyes Kaleb looked at Chase.

"Well pooch," he said picking up HUGGY and smiling. "We better start walking...we got a date with a lawyer and a half chewed teddy bear."

Chase Barked happily and licked Kaleb's face.

Then turning they started the long walk back to town...Together.

HOWDY!

by Norm

We had chatted online for a long time and I knew, more than he, what was in his heart and head. That boy was a puppy, through and through, and it was time to make it a reality.

We had never met, but arranged, finally to get together tonight, at the local leather bar. My goodie bag was packed. I dressed in full Masters leathers, tight leather breeches, tall boots, military cut leather shirt and tie, officer's cap and gloves. Boy was instructed to wear a leather t shirt and leather pants with combat boots.

I waited patiently at a dark table in the corner with my beer. Watching the boys and Sirs play the endless game of "who wants me".

When he walked in, I knew immediately it was him. Eager, puppy energy radiated from his body. Looking quickly from side to side, like a dog let loose in a field. He needed reined in, controlled, and trained.

He went to the bar and got a beer, then began to look around the room. As he got closer to my table I smiled.

"Pup, over here." I called.

All grins, he bounded over to the table and grabbed a hold of me for a hug. Such energy would serve him well.

"Boy, I'm glad to meet you finally." I smiled.

"Sir, thank you for meeting me." he grinned back.

We chatted for a time, catching up on news, getting the feel of each other. We finished our beers and I sent boy to the bar to fetch another round. While he was gone, I went into my bag and pulled out a stainless steel dog dish and set it on the table.

133

As he returned his eyes settled on the gleaming bowl before him. He set the beers down and stared into my eyes. Without a work I picked up one beer and slowly poured it into the bowl. I gave the pup a nod.

"Here Sir? in the bar? Now?" he asked, head darting side to side to see who was watching.

"Boy, you are a pup, you know it. Time to act on your true feelings." I stated matter of fact. "Who cares who is watching?"

He hesitantly looked around again, then quickly gave the beer a quick sniff, and looked around again. Satisfied he was not drawing undo attention; he lowered his head and gave the beer a tentative lap. Then another, and another. Soon the boy was enjoying taking his drink from the bowl, and would come up grinning from ear to ear at me, beer dripping from the corners of his mouth.

"Good pup." was all I needed to say. Now come here and really greet your Master.

He came over and I grabbed a hold of him in a tight embrace.

"Taste your Masters leathers pup, give them a good lick." I instructed.

Pup shot out his tongue and licked at my shirt, slobbering and loving every minute as I held him tight. Pup moved up the chest and was soon to my face where he began to give me big puppy licks, grinning for all he was worth.

"Down pup, good boy." I said laughing.

He backed off and took his seat across from me.

"Pup, we need to talk about what is going to happen to you." I began.
"Sir?" he asked.

"I have plans for you; I want to make your dreams real." I said.
"Sir, you mean my puppy dreams Sir?" he asked with a smile on his face.
"Boy, you know that is what I mean. Are you ready to meet your destiny?

Once I begin, there is not much chance of turning back. I will pursue the goal until it is complete. "I said, staring him right in the eye.

He bowed his head and I detected a tear trailing down his cheek.

"No one has been able to do that Sir; do you think you really can?" he asked, with hope in his eyes.

Without a word, I went back to my bag and pulled out some leather mitts, laying them on the table.

I went back to the bag and pulled out a full leather hood, created to bring a boy completely into the image of a dog. It had a unique gag that would fill the boy's mouth, only allowing him to whimper around it. The center of the gag came out so I could feed the pup without taking the gag out. When the center was removed, the boy could make growling sounds from deep in his throat, but not much else. Was he ready for this?

With the sound of the buckles and locks hitting the table, I laid it there and stared at the boy. Would he really be able to take this step I wondered? Was what he felt only fantasy? Could he turn it into reality?

He looked over the gear for the longest time, and then hesitantly picked it up in trembling hands. He sniffed it, rubbed it, even gave it a quick lick when he thought I wasn't watching.

"You want me to put that on in here Sir? I'm not sure I can in front of all these guys." he whispered.

I said nothing. Just watched the gears turning inside the boy, hoping that the cogs would fit and he could move forward. This was his decision, and probably the hardest one in his life.

"Can I just try it on Sir?" he asked.

"No pup, if that hood goes on, it stays on. Your first "trial" will last 48 hours as a pup. I will then take the hood off and you will have an hour to wash, and decide if you want to continue. The next trial will be for one week. At that time you will have the hood and gear removed and 24 hours as a boy to wash, thinks and make a decision. At that time, the hood goes back on as well as all of your puppy gear, and you remain that way for approximately 2 weeks at a time, for as long as I determine I want you as my pup. Be very clear boy, I do not give in easily to begging and pleas." I said knowing this was the turning point.

He looked at me for a very long time, as his mind wandered in and out of his fantasy, trying to reconcile it with reality. Here it was before him, and he knew he and to make a decision. Tears began to flow down his face, as he began to tear down the walls of boyhood. He was entering the world of human dogs, and knew that is where he belonged. With a small nod, he held out his hands to be fitted with the paws.

"Tell me boy; tell me as a man that this is what you want. "I demanded.

"Sir, make me your pup Sir." was all he said, his eyes pleading with me.

I picked up the mitts and pulled them tightly onto his hands, removing from him all ability to function in a human way.

As I picked up the hood, I asked one more time. "Tell me boy that this is what you want."

The puppy smile was back as he began to flex his new paws. Tears still streamed down his face, but these were tears of joy.

"Make me your pup, Sir."

I loosened the lacing on the hood and worked it down over pups head. It fit well, and began to lace it up tightly. The muzzle looked terrific on him as well as the perky leather ears. He had a difficult time taking the gag, it was large to hold in his mouth. After some struggling, it was in. When I was done lacing, I brought the wide leather collar around and buckled it in the back. I held the lock out for pup to see then without much ceremony, pulled pup toward my chest and reaching around, snapped the lock shut on the buckle. He was now my pup, for at least the next 48 hours.

"Pup, from now on, do not attempt human speech. You will get my attention and communicate with me by barking or whining. Understood?" A sound from somewhere in his throat escaped the gag. If that pup had

had a tail at that moment , it would have been wagging furiously.

I patted my pup on the head and pulled out the last thing in my bag. A leash. I clipped it to the front of the hood, and pulled my new pup out of the darkness of the corner. I paraded that pup around the bar, proud of my new creation.

It was time to leave, to take my pup into his new world. I lead him to the table, grabbed the bag and pulled him out the door. My pick up was just down the street, my new pup happily following. When we got there, he stood near the passengers door.

"No pup, you don't sit in a seat." I stated.

I pulled him to the back were my dog cage was sitting. An old dirty quilt lay inside, piss stained and rank. I opened the cage door and pulled the pup toward it. He balked, having second thoughts about being a dog, but it was too late. I pulled him toward the cage and pushed him in. The lock snapped shut on my pup. His whimpering followed me as I got in the cab and drove away.

When we arrived, I backed the truck into the garage. Moving to the cage, I unlocked the door and pulled out a grateful puppy. From traveling in the old quilt, he now had more of a dog scent to him than a human one. That was good, because it would help "Buck" adjust to his new kennel partner. Without talking I pulled the pup to the far wall of the garage. Here I had a kennel built with a private door to a secluded outdoor run. Buck my black lab was happy to see me.

I opened the door and played with him for a while, letting my "boy pup" watch with confusion and fear in his eyes. I put Buck back in his run and pulled the boy over to my workbench.

Holding him in my arms I whispered in his ears that it was going to be ok, he would adjust and love his new life. As I stroked him with one hand, pressing his face close to my chest, I grabbed a jar of hormone scent from the shelf and rubbed it on his ass.

The smell reached my boy pup and his reaction was that of confusion.

"It's ok boy, this will help you and Buck get aquatinted tonight. Just let go of your human side and embarrass your pup side.

I led him back to the run and opened the door.

"Pup, Buck is going to want to get real friendly with you, I suggest you don't resist."

I pushed the pup in on all fours and laughed as I left the two to get to know each other.

I sat back with a beer, ready to watch the action.

Buck approached the new "bitch" with interest as the boy backed himself into the corner, realizing what was going to happen. The scent was working, and Buck was more than aroused. He barked excitedly and growled at the new member of the kennel. The cage was too small to stand in and with paws, the gag in his mouth there wasn't much he could do. They circled each other until Buck managed to finally get behind the boy. He mounted him forcefully and within a short time his huge dog dick was pressing against the ass of boy pup. He resisted, and tried to get away, but Buck overpowered him. His dick was soon buried deep within the boy's ass. A scream erupted from around the gag, then a series of whimpers. But as Bucks cock grew to fill that space and he worked it in and out, the boy became very aroused. Moans of pleasure began escaping the gag as Buck filled his boy ass with his swollen knob.

Within minutes Buck spewed his dog cum up his ass then rode him until his engorged cock went down enough to pull out.

I was satisfied that the boy and Buck would get along famously this night, so I headed to bed, knowing he was going to get fucked over and over again until morning, when I would pull him out and feed him my dick down his hot throat.

When I headed out to the kennel the next morning, I found my two dogs asleep, Buck's head resting on the boy's rump. The both came immediately awake as I came to the cage door.
"Morning boys, hope you had a good evening." I said.

I shoved a bowl of food in for the lab and pulled the boy out. Attaching a leash, I brought him to my bedroom and had him sit in front of me. "You ok boy?" I asked.

He whined a bit and shook his head yes. I knew he had to be hungry and thirsty but was glad to see he wasn't complaining.

"Well, I am going to take care of you here boy, just hang tight." I smiled. I pulled my jock off and smacked my dick cross the leather covered face of the boy.

"We need to take care of your thirst boy; Dad has some water here for you."

I pulled out the center plug of the gag, and pressed my cock into the hole. A warm stream of piss began to fill the boy's mouth. He gagged and tried not to take it, but there wasn't much choice. Soon it was flowing down his throat and he swallowed without much hesitation.

When I was done, I kept my dick inside the tube, beginning to slide it back and forth, getting harder as I did so. The tube pressed against me and the boys tongue began to caress what penetrated his hot mouth. His eyes lit up as he realized I was going to fuck his face.

I pressed my hot cock deep into his mouth, causing him to gag, but he didn't try to back off. I grabbed a hold of his leathered head and really pumped, until great streams of hot cum filled his mouth. He swallowed eagerly, knowing that I expected him to do so.

Finally I pulled out, leaving my new pup panting. With a smile I shoved the gag back in and told the pup that is was time for him to piss and shit. I led him to the backyard and motioned for him to do his business.

I watched as my new pup tried to figure out where and how to piss. He looked around to see if anyone could see what was happening. Satisfied that this was a very private backyard, he went over to a tree and tried to lift a leg and let a stream go. With some work, pup succeeded. Shitting was another matter. He squatted and tried, but nothing seemed to want to come out.

I went out and attached the leash.

"Well pup, this was your one chance today, but be happy, I will let you try again tomorrow. In the mean time, don't even think about shitting in the house."

I pulled the pup back into the house and led him to my dungeon.

"Pup, as part of your training, you will be in bondage daily. Get use to it." I pulled him to a board on the floor that had many eyebolts all around it. I led him there and had him assume the 'dog position" as I manacled his paws down, his legs tight and his collar up to the ceiling. He was immobile now.

The tit clamps came next, and attached to the board. One move and he would pull on those tender nips. The pup whined, it hurt, but he didn't try to get loose. Those puppy eyes looked up at me and begged, but it didn't change things.

I moved to his ass, and began fingering his hole. He didn't like that much, but there was no way for him to get away.

I went from one finger, to two, then three....all the time lubing his insides, thrusting with as much force as I had in my hand. He bucked and thrashed, but he took it.

I was horny now, watching him struggle, so off came the jock and my hot cock was pressing against his tight boy ass. With one huge thrust, I was in. The boy screamed, but there was not stopping his Master now. I fucked him over and over, until his hot chute brought me to a terrific climax, shooting my hot ropes of cum into his guts.

Reaching over to my table, I brought out another piece of gear, a dog tail. I took the plug and pushed it deep into the pup's ass. He cried out again, and tried to collapse on the board, but the collar chain help him up.

He soon recovered and realized something was different on his backside. I left him there, trying to get control of the tail that was sticking out of his hole.

I left the boy there for most of that day, fucking him, watching him, pissing down his throat. When it came time to remove the hood and allow him to make some decisions, I was torn. Maybe I should just keep him this way, no choice...but I had to know what was going on inside that head.

I pulled out the tail, released him and removed the hood.

It took sometime for the boy to recover, he just wanted to curl up at my feet and rest. I pulled him up, on two legs, and looked him square in the eyes

"Boy....tell me what you want."

For the longest time, he just stared back. Hatred mixed with desire. Emotions raged inside of him.

With difficulty, he replied. "Sir, we have only begun to train me. Please continue."

He held out his hands for the paws to be returned.
I smiled and complied.

ABOUT THE AUTHOR

Michael Daniels is a Leatherman in Ohio. Originally from central Indiana, and back in the Midwest via 5 years in Southern California, he has been involved in BDSM and leather for the past 15+ years, first finding his leather-self as a boy and now on his journey as a Master/Daddy.

As co-creator, webmaster, and president of leatherDOG.com, he has a special interest in human dog training and behavior. Michael lives with his human pups jefpup, boy chuck, and pup taber, and his three real canines.

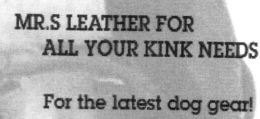

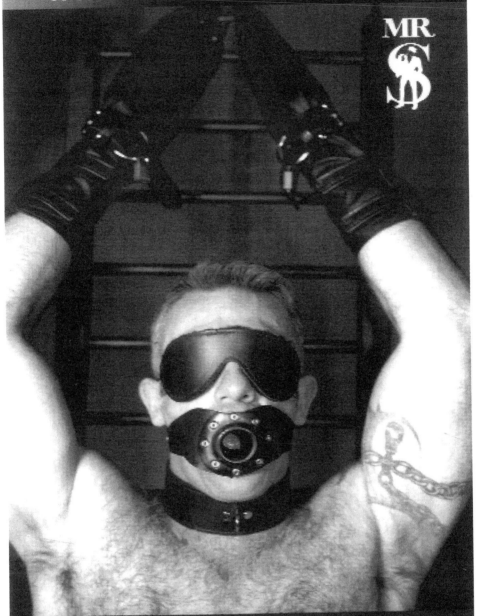

Made in the USA
San Bernardino, CA
27 February 2013